THE VAN GOGH WINDOW

A Novel

ANTHONY MCDONALD

Anchor Mill Publishing

Anchor Mill Publishing

4/04 Anchor Mill

Paisley PA1 1JR

SCOTLAND

anchormillpublishing@gmail.com

Cover design by Barry Creasy

Dedicated to the memory of Tony Linford who, years ago, made me a present of the title 'The Van Gogh Window'. He also made me a present of his love, and of his life.

ONE

It was soon after my divorce from Anne that I began to dream about Happy. And after that I started to think about him. About that year at Durham…

Anne and Happy had both come into my life at the same time. At the same moment of the same day.

I'd had a premonition beforehand. Returning to university to begin my second year, and at the very moment when the land fell away beneath the train to reveal Durham's cathedral rearing over the grovelling rooftops, I was suddenly certain that this year would be different. The certainty was so strong that I felt it physically: a tingling in the bloodstream. That year – nine years ago now – I would meet the person or people who would shape my life.

Or some of them. Or some of it.

Anne appeared in the street beneath my window the next morning. A new room, looking into the street from the second floor, and new voices down there, outside. 'Who can we call on for coffee this term? Everyone's moved.' I put my head out of the window and looked down. They were three girls and a boy, though you were supposed to think: *women* and *man*. They looked all right and I had five mugs.

'Call on me,' I said. 'I'm David.' Even in those days my occasional bursts of spontaneity tended to have far-reaching consequences.

It became a ritual. Every time they had a ten o'clock in the history lecture hall next door they would follow it with coffee in my room. Sometimes all four came, sometimes just two or three. Never only one. That was an unspoken taboo but strictly observed. Solo visits would have changed everything, giving rise to relationships where, for now, only a social situation existed.

They had names of course. There was Janie, forever knitting an endless scarf for her boyfriend, and Laura, already a comforting, aunt-like figure at nineteen. There was Anne, the pretty one, the witty one, and there was Happy.

'Why do people call him Happy?'

'A spelling mistake when he was little, apparently. His real name's Harry, short for Henry though it isn't any shorter, but the other version stuck. But you should know that. He's in your college after all. I'm surprised you haven't bumped into him before.'

'I wasn't very outgoing last year,' I said.

'Wake up, David.' It was Anne speaking. The others would not have talked to me like this – at least, not so soon. 'Or university will be over and nothing'll have happened.'

Anne had been a shrewd observer if a poor prophet. I had been virtually untouched, unaltered by my first year away from home, remaining shy, virginal, conceited. I'd looked at Anne and wondered for the first time if it would be through her that change would come.

*

I had to tell people about the divorce from Anne, of course. It was all done by letter in those days. (We got divorced in early '89.) I wrote to Malcolm, among other people. I'd done my teacher training with Malcolm. But he'd chucked it in a few years afterwards and moved to Paris. Malcolm was gay, I had now learnt. I don't know whether he moved to Paris because he was gay or whether he was gay because he'd moved to Paris. At any rate he now had a boyfriend there who was called Henri. Henri was nineteen. Malcolm – who, like me, was twenty-eight – taught English to French businessmen at one of the larger business schools.

Malcolm's response to my news surprised me. It was startling almost, but also heart-warming. He rang me up and asked me if I'd like to go on holiday with him. He was going to Provence in three days' time. The boyfriend, Henri, couldn't go. He, Malcolm, would like some company, and he guessed a break might do me good. I was between jobs, as they say. I was so surprised by Malcolm's offer that I said yes. I just needed to get myself to Paris the day after next, he told me. Stay the night with him and Henri, then travel onward with Malcolm from there. I phoned and booked a flight from Heathrow to Charles de Gaulle. Then I started packing. Not that I'd need many clothes. It was early July and I was heading south. I started sorting things out, tracking down my passport, things like that. And as I did all that my mind kept going back to the days when I knew Happy.

TWO

Winter had come down hard that second year at Durham. All through January the green-grey ice-floes had sailed down the river, under Framwellgate Bridge, past the boathouses, round the horseshoe bend. Some had tumbled, smashing, over the weir to disappear under Crossgate and out of the city's sight while others lodged at the rim, backing up as the days passed to form a crust which froze together at the joins. This new skin the river wore was rough and lumpy as an alligator's and at night when the streets were still it could be heard squeaking under its own pressure, a sound which seemed to flitter around the valley like a summer evening's bats. 'Do you think it would be possible?' asked Happy, 'to walk across it?'

'Possible perhaps,' said Anne, putting down her coffee, 'but don't ask me to join you if you try it.'

'David will,' said Happy flatly, not even looking up.

'You should see Happy's lecture notes today,' said Laura. 'They're all seals.'

Happy's lecture notes were unlike most people's: they consisted not of written words but pictures. His surprised neighbours in the lecture room would watch designs and figures taking shape in response to a chance word in the lecture: stream of consciousness doodling, or perhaps a stream of the unconscious. I thought Happy one of the least conscious people I had met. He spoke little and seemed to wear his thick mop of hair like an insulator for the brain, protecting it from external stimulus. He was a good draughtsman though; no doubt about that.

'Show David, go on,' Laura coaxed.

Without a word Happy handed the morning's drawings over. He seemed neither reluctant nor pleased to do so; they were just there. Take them or leave them, the silence implied. That morning's lecture on the development of the royal household in medieval England had given rise to three pages of pictures of seals – of the animal rather than the Great or Privy variety. There were real seals and surreal seals, seals swimming, seals dining at restaurant tables, seals peering from the treetops, seals on the cathedral roof. Yesterday it had been grasshoppers. There was not a word of text. God help him when he came to revise, I thought. Then the possibility struck me that Happy could not actually write. In which case, how had he got to university? I'd dismissed that line of thought while Happy put the pictures away. Neither of us spoke. I'd thought the drawings brilliantly executed but pointless and their creator odd without being really interesting.

It was that day that the snow had come.

It had come hesitantly at first but with increasing firmness of purpose as the afternoon wore on. At first each flake formed an island of white on Durham's dark pavements but soon the image was reversed, as the pavement outside my window was reduced to islands of black: the footprints of the students (few other people used the street) who passed and re-passed in intermittent, alternating streams. I watched, seated at my desk. The spectacle provided as good an excuse as any to postpone the start of the essay on Shakespeare's clowns that I was due to hand in two days hence. As usual the road took longer to vanish than the pavement because of traffic but here the traffic was light and soon the time came when the double yellow lines had gone for good. I liked to see this as a watershed; the moment marked the end of the rule of law and the beginning of the snow's anarchic reign. Now you could park your car anywhere you liked, if you had a car, that was. I didn't, of course. In time, if the snow kept on long enough, the cars would be gone too and everything would be as it had been a hundred years ago. Eventually the cathedral and castle would be covered also, and I with them, in a return to a featureless, timeless age of ice. But that was going too far, even for me. I drew the curtains, as it was getting dark, and set to work on Shakespeare's clowns.

In the morning it was perfect. The snow had turned the clock back just the right amount, neither too little nor too far. The cars had gone but not the castle. I made my way across the green to college breakfast. I'd got up earlier than usual and all was dark and still, the few lines of footprints that preceded my own not devaluing too greatly the quality of the scene. With a breath-like sound a quantity of snow slid from the branch of a bush, dislodged by a bird which, breast deep, now flopped away. A few parked cars it was true, intruded like donkeys on the green but they were so comprehensively wrapped in white as not to count. The cathedral stood out against the southern sky, the castle against the northern, and as, minute by minute, the light increased it picked out every buttress, every gargoyle, every dripstone and edged them in white while hiding every dustbin, drain-cover and fire hydrant: the twentieth-century clutter swept away, the old enhanced.

The castle was the principal building of my college – my own room was in a modern annexe – and it was approached from the green through a Norman gatehouse which opened onto a central court. It would have been convenient to call this court a quad but that name was ruled out by its shape, the grass plot in its centre being round. Even the notice forbidding you to walk on it was whited out. Arguably it was without authority that day: it said Keep Off The Grass, not off the snow. Now, as I straightened after ducking through the postern gate I saw a figure standing on the forbidden whiteness. I walked nearer and saw with some surprise that it was Happy, smoking a cigarette.

'Want one?' Happy held the packet out.

'Before breakfast? Thank you, no. Couldn't you sleep?'

Happy had the reputation of a late riser. If he made it to breakfast at all he would arrive at the tail end when most other people had left.

'I just like to see it look like this,' Happy answered, 'if only for one morning of the year, before it gets spoilt.'

'I know. And look, it's starting now.' I nodded towards the postern where young people were beginning to stream in, laughing and pursued by snowballs.

'Enough,' said Happy. 'Come on. Let's go inside.' We moved off, up the steps and into the Great Hall where, because Happy habitually sat at one table under the portrait of Bishop Van Mildert, while I always sat at the one over which Bishop Tunstall hung, our paths diverged as abruptly as they had just crossed.

It was eleven o'clock in the evening and I had just put the finishing touches to Shakespeare's clowns. I was either about to take off my shoes or to clean my teeth – I had not yet decided on the order of ceremonies – when there was a knock at the door. I said, 'Come in,' without surprise. Neighbours, seeing your light on, were apt to pop in at any hour of the evening for a chat. But tonight my visitor was Happy, wearing a duffel coat, an Everton scarf and a woolly bobble-hat pulled down over his ears.

'Come for a walk,' he said.

'A what?'

'A walk,' Happy repeated matter-of-factly. 'Down by the river. It's snowed again. You'll like it.'

I was more than surprised. I thought the suggestion crazy. But I was unable quickly to find a good reason to refuse 'I'm just going to bed' might seem reasonable enough to older people but it was a lame excuse at nineteen and soon I heard my own voice saying, 'OK. If you like. Why not?'

Soon we had descended the steps that ran down between St. Chad's College and Dunelm Bridge and found ourselves at the bottom of the wooded gorge where the river ran, its presence taken on trust tonight since its sharp-edged surface was buried beneath a thick white quilt. The ice had stopped squeaking a day or two before; it was now locked tight. There was no movement to be heard or seen or felt. Without speaking we turned along the towpath towards the horseshoe bend.

Happy broke the silence when we got there. 'What do you think of it?' He seemed to be inviting my appreciation of something he had made himself: one of his pictures perhaps, or a newly decorated room.

'It suits me,' I said.

Happy seemed not to find my reply an odd one. He said, 'That's what I thought. I thought it when I saw you this morning. Before that I didn't know....' The phrase tailed away. 'Like celestial Tippex,' he said a moment or two later. Then, 'Are you in love with Anne?'

'I don't think so.' I was following easily Happy's changes of tack: so easily that it surprised me. 'Are you?'

'I don't think so either,' Happy said, 'and yet....'

That was the full extent of our discussion of the subject but it seemed somehow to have gone deeper than the many conversations on the theme of love that I and my other friends indulged in and that often lasted hours. It now occurred to me for the first time in my life that the words people said to one another might bear no more than a passing resemblance to what they were trying to communicate.

After that, conversation began to flow more easily. Ideas began to link up, sentences sometimes even to end. We talked about our childhood days, Happy's in the country, mine in the town. We were surprised to discover how much we had in common, not knowing yet that you could find as much in common as you wished with anyone you chose, provided that you wanted to. Yet somehow it seemed to matter.

We turned the horseshoe bend. Here the wooded banks rose more steeply above us, bearing up tier upon tier of trees, their scaffold of branches just visible in the dim rays of the lamps on Prebends' Bridge. The whole composition was finished with a white haze of frosted twigs, a three-dimensional latticework of infinite complexity.

'Like life, really,' said Happy, reflecting on precisely that but not bothering to check whether I understood him. 'Can you climb trees?'

'I used to. But it's a few years since...'

'Race you to the top of that sycamore.'

I would not have recognized a sycamore even in daylight and with its leaves on but Happy was blithely shinning up a nearby trunk and for a second time that evening I could find no good reason not to follow. To my surprise it was quite easy, like the dangerous feats performed in dreams, and soon we had both climbed as high as we could without breaking the slender branches we stood on. The tree was already waving about alarmingly in response to the smallest movement either of us made. 'I wonder how that couple managed to do it in a pear tree,' Happy said.

'Which couple?'

'You know. The couple in Chaucer. In the Miller's Tale.'

'Oh, right,' I said. 'I've wondered that myself. I never knew historians could read, though.' I raised my eyebrows in mock surprise. 'Read literature, I mean.'

'Supercilious bastard,' said Happy and shook the tree. 'I did English for A-level as it happens. Economics too, if you're interested.'

'German and French,' I countered and then, with no qualifications left to hurl, we each tried to shake the other from his perch. Half a minute later we were on the ground again having neither exactly fallen nor scrambled down but something in between.

We lit cigarettes in a futile attempt to warm hands that were now stinging with cold and walked on. The weir was eerily silent except at the narrow fish passes where a little water spilled down from beneath the icy cap as if to remind us that it could not be stilled completely or for ever. Here we struck matches and flicked them out across the river's flat expanse. They blazed a second like shooting stars, lighting up the snow as they arc-ed towards it, then the white swallowed them and turned to blackness. At last the matchbox, as well as Happy's cigarette packet, was empty. Without anything having to be said we knew the walk was over. We climbed the path beneath the cathedral's massive silhouette and parted on the green, Happy to his turret somewhere in the castle, I to my more conventional, modern room. It seemed to me at that moment, nine years ago, that all thought and all feeling had been banished from my mind except a sense of peace; that the internal as well as the external landscape had been whited out by Happy's celestial Tippex.

THREE

There was a flight you could take from London to Paris that was operated by Air India. A Boeing 747 used to fly into Heathrow from Bombay, then a few hours later the same plane flew out from Charles de Gaulle to Delhi. In between, cheap tickets were offered to anyone who wanted to make the short hop between the European capitals.

I thought it would be fun. With any luck they'd serve a decent curry on board…

They did no such thing. This was low cost flying before low cost flying had been invented, and the London Paris leg coincided with the cabin crew's rest break. They lay prostrate with exhaustion across rows of empty seats while the Boeing lumbered slowly into the air and bumped its way along the cloud corridor. The journey was so short and the old Boeing's rate of climb so gentle that I realised we wouldn't even climb to cruising height before it was time to descend into Paris. My mind went back to that snowy winter nine years before…

*

There were seven degrees of acquaintanceship at university, each one signalled by its own social convention. There were the people you nodded to in the street, the people you said hallo to and those you would cross the street to speak to. Then – number four – came the people whose rooms you might visit casually but only in the company of someone else (your girlfriend's best friend and your best friend's girlfriend were in this category) and there were those whom you would call on at any time, alone or not, for any good reason such as to discuss an essay topic or to borrow milk. This group, embracing most of your neighbours and a sizeable chunk of your department as well, was a rather large one. The sixth degree consisted of those on whose doors you would knock for no reason whatever and who in their turn would not expect your visit to have anything so prosaic as a purpose. A small group this. Finally, number seven, a plane of relationship not restricted to university but to which neither I nor Happy had yet attained, was the one which usually has room besides yourself for one person only.

Happy's late evening visit and the snowy ramble that followed it had abruptly shifted our relationship from group four to group six, missing out the large fifth group in between. My room was easily accessible, lying on the main axes between the university library, the castle, the cathedral and the shops. Happy's, by contrast, was approached by a flight of ninety steps and lay in the innermost recesses of the castle on the way to nowhere else. The room was an unusual shape: bottle-shaped, Happy called it – you entered along the neck.

In good weather the view from the window was superb. Today it was just a blur of white, its only prominent feature a building from the previous century – a period Happy called the Age of Endarkenment – a hundred of whose windows peered up at Happy's. You never saw a light turned off to indicate the migration of occupants from one room to another and when the city suffered a power cut that windowed wall became a beacon in the blackness. It was the county gaol. It was Happy's grim joke to peer from his window in the evening, indicate the lights to whoever his visitor might be and, with a sardonic smile, exclaim, 'Oh look. The prisoners are in.'

The walls of Happy's room were mainly covered with reproductions of famous paintings but right above his bed two texts in his own handwriting were blue-tacked. One was a quotation from Machiavelli which read: 'The Prince should read History'. Reading history was what Happy was here for and he did it with about as much enthusiasm as he might have picked oakum. He had selected the text for his own encouragement. The other one was more cryptic; it read: 'This is not Dungeness'. I asked him to explain it. He said that Dungeness was a windswept shingle beach in Kent: something I already knew. Pressed further, he explained that the phrase was a quote from a dream he had once had – an idea that intrigued me. My own dreams, though occasionally memorable, were never sources of quotation.

'I've never been there,' Happy said, 'though I dream of the place often. I can't think why. It's a dismal spot by all accounts. And by the way, there's nothing wrong with quoting your dreams, or even your waking thoughts. I recommend it to you. If ever I write a sentence in an essay that seems more apt or prettier than usual I stick inverted commas at either end. Somehow it seems to commend itself more to the tutors that way. They never ask where a quotation comes from. They want you to think they know the source of all quotations. History is bluff.'

'University is bluff,' I'd said.

'And life itself.'

'Life yes. Art no.'

Our conversations usually came round to art in the end, often specifically to painting, a subject that stirred Happy to a rare degree of enthusiasm. 'I once thought I had the makings of a good painter,' he explained. 'Only the ambition went away and the talent was probably never there in the first place. Now all I have left are opinions.' Which were sometimes curious.

'Look at the *Marriage of Arnolfini* next time you're in the National,' he said. 'In the background is a mirror on the wall. People say the reflection in it is the artist's. It isn't though; it's yours. Try it and see.'

Months later I'd gone to look. The minute reflection had not been wearing my clothes that day but the face, a single brush-blob, might have been my own. It was a nice idea. Not far from Arnolfini, though, I'd come upon Botticelli's *Portrait of a Young Man* and discovered with a shock that it resembled Happy. Had he been there, I now thought, Happy might have countered that the picture looked like every man of nineteen and that that was its genius. But Happy had not been there and the resemblance had hurt.

It was in the realm of music though, that I'd held views of my own. In Happy's room we listened to Beethoven, in mine to Schubert – in addition to the pop music of the day which was the same everywhere. But it was over Beethoven that we disagreed. When Happy wanted to provoke me he would put the finale of the Ninth Symphony on the turntable and turn the volume up.

'It's rubbish,' I would say. 'Self-conscious, overblown, bombastic...'

'Any more adjectives?' Happy would enquire placidly.

'Triumphalist...'

Happy would silence me with a well-aimed pillow.

'One day,' Happy said simply, 'you will change your mind. Everyone comes to love Beethoven in the end.'

'Bollocks,' I said.

'But how?' Happy went on, ignoring me, almost to himself. 'That is the question. How will you get there and with who?'

'With whom,' I corrected.

These conversations would fizzle out under pressure from the music. In any case it wasn't considered cool to remain articulate for too long at a stretch.

Once, but only once, we talked about our dreams. At that time I was fascinated by dreams, especially my own. I recounted a recent and particularly pleasant one to Happy. I had been walking in sunshine in a village ringed with trees where birds sang and children played. The dream had lasted a considerable time, or seemed to. The details had been fine and compelling. I finished describing it, then asked, 'And what did you dream last night? Dungeness again, or don't you remember?'

'Oh I remember all right,' said Happy.

'Tell me then.'

'You don't want to hear it.'

'Of course I do,' I said.

'Well then. I'm afraid it was shorter and more brutal than yours, though. I dreamed you shot me through the head.'

*

I was brought back to myself by the voice of a stewardess telling me that we were landing, and would I please do my seat belt up.

FOUR

Malcolm had told me to take the RER underground service as far as the Gare du Nord, and then change onto the older, slower Métro. I would get off at Place Blanche, by the Moulin Rouge. I was looking forward to seeing Paris again. I hadn't been there since I was a teenager. But even now I had to wait, as I ploughed through the city's chalky subsoil, looking blankly at the black reflections in the window of my underground train. With nothing more real to distract me, my thoughts went back to Durham again.

*

The snow was going. The real world was returning to the city streets. It was the world, as Happy put it, '...of yellow lines and parking fines and meter maids all in a row.' The quotes are his. We were all having eleven o'clock coffee in my room.

'Anyone fancy some theatre this afternoon?' Anne asked.

'The Assembly Rooms, do you mean?' Happy asked, puzzled. 'I didn't think there was anything on this week. Or do you mean in Newcastle?'

'Neither,' said Anne. 'I mean the Court House. The Bloody Assizes. Not that they call them assizes any more. But we ought to go and have a look anyway. Part of our education.'

Happy said that he would not go, Laura that she would. Janie, still knitting her incessant scarf, said that she would go: it was sure to be fascinating. I said that I too would join the party but on condition that Janie did not take the scarf. I drew the line, I remember saying, at sitting next to a *tricoteuse*.

The court room was not unlike the Assembly Rooms, which were the principal venue for student drama, in that both were decked out with impressive quantities of brass rail and red plush. But the court was intimate in the extreme, far smaller than I'd expected. Reaching down from the public gallery I could almost have removed the barristers' wigs had I been tempted to. I was not. But the shortage of space did not prevent the onstage action achieving an intensity rarely found at the Assembly Rooms. Here, the author of the entertainment was life itself; life the subject matter too, along with death.

When we arrived the judge was summing up a case that had been carried over from the previous day. An elderly man was in the dock, listening alertly, sometimes nodding in agreement. One bandaged wrist, prominently displayed on the dock rail testified to a half-hearted suicide attempt the night before. It appeared that he had formed the habit of firing a shotgun at his neighbours, later at the postman, and finally at the policeman who was sent round to have a word. He was on trial for attempted murder. The judge suggested that the jury consider the prisoner's mental state, then sent them out to find a verdict.

'Exciting, don't you think?' said Janie. I murmured a reluctant agreement, wondering whether excitement was really what you ought to feel, this being real life after all. Then my attention was taken up by the entrance of a second jury, new white-wigged counsels for defence and prosecution, a new prisoner in the dock. Surveying the new cast my eye fell suddenly on Happy, seated a few places away. I was doubly surprised because I hadn't heard anyone enter the public gallery and because Happy had said that he wouldn't come. He was looking away when I spotted him so no glance of greeting was exchanged. And I was too awed by my surroundings to call out.

The new case concerned a closing-time brawl. A skinhead had been kicked to death. Another one, in a suit, stood in the dock charged with his murder. More skinheads in suits testified in his defence. A few ritual thrusts and parries were exchanged by the barristers and occasionally the judge made a little joke when he judged the tension in need of easing. Soon he was summing up. I was amazed at the speed of the proceedings.

The second jury left, the first returned. Not guilty, was their verdict on the old man. A wave of good feeling swept the court room, a taut balloon of tension punctured. Indefinite detention in a psychiatric institution, said the judge. Nobody seemed to hear.

Like weathermen on a barometer, or like a Greek chorus working shifts, that jury left only to be replaced by the second. Their discussion of the skinhead had been brief. Manslaughter, yes, they said but murder, no. There were audible sounds of relief. I found that my own relief was slightly tinged with disappointment. I'd been cheated of my first sighting of a murderer in the flesh. The judge prescribed a prison term with the easy nonchalance of a doctor ordering a rest-cure. 'There's too much of this putting the boot in, as it's called, about,' he said. That night another of Happy's prisoners would be in.

The scenery was set for a third case. Now it was another impeccably dressed but even younger man who occupied the dock. His age was given as nineteen. He was a bank clerk who had been supplementing his income by offering his body for rent. But the renting process had gone horribly wrong, one of his clients demanding money from him in return for certain photographs not finding their way to his parents or to the bank where he worked. The blackmailer had grown greedy and raised the price. The boy, grown desperate, had strangled him with a silk scarf.

'You have heard the charge against you,' said the judge. 'How do you plead?'

The boy replied so softly that heads craned forward to hear him. 'Guilty, my lord,' he breathed, and in those words that so faintly broke the silence the fall of a sparrow could be heard by straining ears.

'You have pleaded guilty to the crime of murder,' said the judge in a voice now grave and sad. 'There is only one sentence that the law allows: that you be imprisoned for life.' The prisoner, who had appeared among them for no more than two minutes, the sparrow in the feasting hall, was led down steps behind the dock, down steps where the imagination could not follow, and out of sight.

I was aghast. I'd been rewarded for my patience with this glimpse of a murderer and it had not been at all what I'd expected. I looked towards where Happy sat but his seat was empty. A door on the far side of the gallery was just closing.

*

But now we were gliding to a stop at Place Blanche Métro station. I got up and unhooked the silver catch that allowed the door to open. It whooshed and clunked as it did so, and I got out.

FIVE

I made my way up the rue Lepic. Malcolm had told me that it was shaped like a sickle, though a left-handed one. The short straight handle bit climbed past the stage door of the Moulin Rouge and a line of wonderful foodie shops opposite. Malcolm's flat was halfway around the curving 'blade' of the street, higher up. The tip of the rue Lepic poked its way into the picturesque quarter of Montmartre at the top.

It was quite a climb, and though it was early evening by now the sun was still hot, but the street was so attractive that I didn't mind that. I pressed the buzzer and a few seconds later I heard Malcolm's welcoming voice and the buzz and click as he opened the postern gate. The postern gate. That took me back…

Malcolm met me at the top of his flight of stairs. We went into his big salon and I was immediately gobsmacked. It was like walking into an explosion of colour and light. First was the view out of the big window. The sun was pouring into it from the south-west, and I found myself looking out across the roofs of the city towards the Eiffel Tower, which reared up in the distance. But inside the room the sun lit brilliant pictures everywhere I looked. I knew the pictures well. It was as if someone had taken an expensive book of Van Gogh reproductions, dismembered it and plastered the pages all over the walls. When I asked him, Malcolm confirmed that this was actually the case. There were sunflowers here, sunsets there, fields of ripening wheat, the orange roofs of Auvers, the blazing blues of canal and sky at Arles. In Malcolm's flat, especially with the evening sun streaming into it, the effect was overwhelming: a battering of the senses. But what struck me more than that was a memory that came back. I suddenly remembered that Happy's room at university had been similarly decorated, his endarkened castle quarters enlightened by an, admittedly more modest, set of Van Gogh prints. How could I have forgotten that?

'I found it like this when I got back from work this evening,' Malcolm explained. 'It's Henri's doing.' Shyly he added, 'It's my birthday. Today I'm as old as you are, David. Twenty-eight'

'Why the hell didn't you say...?' I made standard apologetic noises about cards and presents. I was glad I'd bought a bottle of wine from the Nicolas shop at the bottom of the street, at least.

'Never mind all that. Look, we've got to call by the café to borrow some more cutlery. There's two other people coming as well and I don't have enough knives and forks.'

'Oh,' I said, 'that'll be nice.' I meant the other guests.

'Well,' Malcolm explained. 'Henri got a bit carried away in the market this morning. He bought a whole pike. It's one helluva big pike. *Le brochet au beurre blanc de la Loire.* Henri's in charge of the preparations, thank God. Where is he?' He looked away towards an unseen kitchen. *'Henri, viens! Laisse ton sacré poisson!'* Come here. Leave your bloody fish.

Henri emerged from the kitchen along the corridor. *'Voilà,'* he said, *'ça y est. Bonjour, David.'* And he sniffed at his fingers before giving me his hand to shake.

It was a convivial evening. The other guests were a gay couple, one English, one French, called Peter and Fabrice. We talked a mixture of the two languages. We talked about Van Gogh. With that lot plastered over the walls we could hardly not have done. I said that the view from the window here reminded me of a painting by Van Gogh: the one in which the Eiffel Tower appears half built.

'It should do,' Malcolm said. 'It was painted from the house next door, which was where he lived with his brother Theo when he first came to Paris.'

Peter said that when *he*'d first arrived in Paris two years before there had been an attic window visible from his flat that shed a yellow light at night. Against the blue dark it had reminded him of windows in paintings by Van Gogh.

'I hope you like Van Gogh,' Malcolm said to me. 'Because this holiday we're going on is partly to

27

follow his footsteps to Provence.'

'I'm up for that,' I said. 'I've always been a fan of Vincent's. I had a friend at university whose walls were plastered with Van Gogh prints. I'd forgotten that till I saw yours when I arrived here. My friend's name was Happy,' I said. For some reason I found it was imperative just then to get that out, to speak his name.

'Intriguing name,' said Malcolm. 'Was he? Happy by nature as well as name, I mean.'

'Not at the end,' I said. 'Tell you sometime.' We had a fortnight.

Henri was a charming boy. He was very ... I suppose I'd have to say pretty. Perhaps that was fair enough. He was gay after all, and only just nineteen. Big almond-shaped brown eyes, and full lips. He wouldn't be joining his partner and me on this Provence jaunt, he explained, because his mother liked him to spend a week with her every summer in the spa town of Vichy. It was a bit dull, he said, but he loved his mother and still did this every year. He was an only child and his father was dead.

'He's very good to her,' Malcolm explained. 'Sees her every weekend and cooks her lunch.'

I was enjoying the pike with white butter sauce enormously. I thought Henri's mother was lucky to have a son who could cook like that.

After the guests had gone and the washing-up had

been incarcerated in the dishwasher, Henri took himself off to bed.

Malcolm poured himself and me a final cognac. 'Holiday begins tonight,' he said. We sat beneath the Van Gogh paintings and talked.

'I want to hear about your friend Happy,' Malcolm said. That surprised me a bit. I'd only mentioned his name once.

I told him the whole story, up to the point where we were in the court room and Happy left. I sighed involuntarily. 'And I'm afraid I only saw him one more time after that. I don't feel very good about it.'

'Tell me,' said Malcolm, in the gentle voice that people use when coaxing forth reminiscences over the third cognac.

'It was later that same evening,' I said. 'I was well behind with my weekly essay and I was having trouble concentrating. That wasn't surprising. The events of the court room, the sentencing to life imprisonment of someone my own age, someone who had stood literally within touching distance but was now a murderer – all this had taken my imagination over and rather monopolised it. Even at dinner I'd found it hard to eat. I'd been impressed by the professionalism of the judge. (He lodged in the castle's state rooms while the court was sitting, and dined at high table with the dons.) There he was, cheerfully tucking into pheasant pie, the business of the day firmly behind him after six o'clock.

And I wasn't surprised, finally, when Happy knocked at my door around eleven o'clock. "Can we talk?" he asked me. "About this afternoon?"

'"Yes,"I said. "I want to very much. But not just now. Tomorrow. Tomorrow all day if you like. But..." I pointed to my unfinished essay. "Deadline nine a.m."

'"I understand," Happy said. He left and softly closed the door behind him.

'I made some coffee, trying to rebuild my concentration. I put a record on the turntable. I even remember what it was. One of my all-time favourites: Schubert's *Winterreisse*. I played the whole of it – all three sides – by which time the essay was as finished as it would ever be. It was nearly two o'clock. I went to bed.' I stopped for a second. 'I remember it in so much detail,' I said, wondering at myself a bit.

'It was obviously important,' Malcolm said. 'The *Winterreisse* is the one where the lovelorn boy drowns himself in the millstream, isn't it?'

'Oh my God,' I said. 'You know that!'

'Anyway, what happened?' Malcolm asked. 'Though I think I can guess. After you told Happy to get lost he did just that?'

'In a manner of speaking, yes,' I answered slowly. 'The morning came as it always does. The history group didn't have a ten o'clock so I didn't expect to see Happy early on. I had lectures myself till twelve in the English department on the other side of town. I walked back the long way round – along the river bank. It wasn't quite spring yet, but birds were making a racket and there was a feeling that things were about to happen. I saw two policemen talking together in the trees on the other side of the river but I didn't think anything of it. I was feeling really great for some reason. You know, one of those days you get when you feel about a hundred and ten per cent. I walked up to the castle and went in to lunch. Do you remember that college lunch feeling? You went in and, in a way that almost knocked the breath out of you, There Was Everybody.'

Malcolm nodded his head.

'That day it was more than that. As I walked in I had the sensation that in that roar, the sound of four hundred people all talking at once, there was only one topic of conversation. Not only was everybody talking but they were all saying the same thing. By the time I got to my usual place I think I knew that one of us – I mean someone from the university – had been fished out of the river. Dead. By the time I sat down I knew it was someone from our own college. I asked who. As if I needed telling. "Paddy Laughton," someone said. "Chap who used to run everywhere, you never saw him walking. Reads history…" And I remember the bloke trying to correct the tense.

'"Not Paddy," I said. "His name was...." only, his name being the one it was, I couldn't manage to say it and had to leave the room. The soup was just arriving. It was mushroom.'

Very gently, Malcolm reached across and touched me on the shoulder. 'And what happened then?'

I said, and it sounded silly as I heard my words come out. 'I married Anne.'

'Incredible!' said Malcolm. 'Just like that? Before the soup?' As well he might.

SIX

Anne had been so practical that first day, so sensible, so right. She was very upset herself by the news of Happy's death but she sensed somehow that my distress was of a different order to her own. Rather than discuss, painfully and uselessly, events and feelings for which neither of us had words, she asked me to embark with her on a very overdue spring cleaning of the flat she shared. It was probably lucky that there was so much to do. The carpets hadn't been taken out and beaten in the memory of the present occupants; there were chests and cupboards which had not been moved or swept behind for years. We actually found some dirty plates at the back of the cooker that Anne had never seen before. They were so encrusted with ancient grime that we threw them in the dustbin.

Happy had left no note, no explanation. The coroner recorded a verdict of accidental death. There was no evidence that it was anything else. That he had been upset the last time I'd seen him? What good could it do anyone to bring that up? That he had dreamed I shot him? I'd watched as a trunk containing Happy's things was loaded onto a lorry in the Castle Court. What would his parents do with the contents? I'd wondered. And who were they? Another month or two and I might have met them. Now I never would. Where did they live, anyway? Colchester, was it? Chelmsford? Ipswich? Somewhere down there. I only knew for certain that it was not Dungeness. Nothing but nothing of Happy remained to me. Addresses were normally only exchanged at the ends of terms, holiday post-cards only after that. It was as if in his own death Happy had cut something away from me and caused me to die a little as well. This was not Dungeness. That negative was all I knew…

I gave Malcolm a slightly edited account of that. He got up and poured us one more cognac. I didn't tell him the next bit…

*

A terrible depression had seized me as the spring advanced. Brighter the weather might grow day by day but blacker and deeper the hole I seemed to be falling down. The doctor prescribed some pills. They made me feel even more disconnected. Anne came to see me but seemed to sit outside. It was the same with all of them: with my college friends, with Laura and Janie. Even when Anne sat on the bed beside me, an arm around my shoulder, she seemed to be outside.

One day she lost patience with me, told me my depression had become self-indulgent, that it served no useful purpose; I had to put the past behind me and get on with life. I became angry with her, told her she didn't understand. A shouting match began and then, suddenly, a frenzy took hold of me; it was something I'd never experienced before. I found myself yelling, swearing, throwing things at Anne. She fled screaming from the room. I saw her from the window, a small figure in the street below. There was something I had to tell her, but what was it? I'm sorry? No. I love you? Something to do with Happy? Or, I hate? My fists were clenched now. They went through the plate-glass as if through butter, and the glass slid down the air like the floe ice down the weir, all shining shards that tinkled softly as they landed. Anne's figure ran from sight, blood ran from my hands, other knuckles hammered at my door.

It was probably the long wait in casualty, with roughly bandaged wrists, that had brought me back to my senses.

Months passed before I made contact again with Anne. It came about through Laura. 'What are you going to do about Anne?' she said one day while Janie's needles clicked away in the corner of the room.

'Do?' I asked.

'Yes, do! Or have you been expecting her to reappear with flowers and apologies?'

'Of course not,' I said. 'I just don't expect she'll want to be reminded of my existence, that's all.'

'The difference between not wanting to see someone again and knowing that it's not your move is enormous. Did you know that? What about writing, at least?'

I'd looked sharply at Laura. Nearby, Janie's knitting

needles clicked on impassively, not missing a beat. 'Are you here as Anne's messenger?' I'd asked.

'No,' said Laura. 'I'm here as yours.'

In the end I called at Anne's flat and, without preamble or flowers, boldly proposed taking a long walk together the next Saturday. Rather to my surprise she, equally bold, accepted at once.

The day was beautiful. It was June. Larks sang overhead as we left the city behind and headed out across an open rolling landscape. We saw hares, alert on distant knolls, that in turn followed our progress with tele-photo vision. We walked into an old mining village, a slimmed-down version of its former self, where the remaining cottages overlooked a wide sun trap of a green. Here one building only stood, the village pub, and there we sat outside, eating sandwiches and drinking beer, at rustic tables made from old ale casks.

Later we lay together at the edge of a field and, under a cloudless sky, partly undressed and made love for the first time. A rite of passage, this, that I'd long tried to imagine, script, cast and direct but the reality was better, easier and more natural than anything I could have wished. It happened as smoothly as I'd slipped my hand through the plate-glass window. And I realised that it was then this rite of passage had occurred – not now but at the moment when my fist broke through the pane. What happened now, so easy, so beautiful, so right, was simply that the rest of me had followed suit…

*

I could see Malcolm looking at me oddly. I must have been silent for a while. I think he could see that I'd skipped a bit. I resumed.

'I moved out of college in my third year and into Anne's flat. It surprised none of our friends. Once it was an accomplished fact it seemed as inevitable as the completion of Janie's endless scarf. She did eventually finish it; it was seven metres long and was worn round the neck of a man she had met when the scarf was only inches long. She married him when it reached eleven feet.

'We got married the next summer. Honeymoon in Italy, return to Durham in the autumn. I began my post-graduate teaching course... And the rest you know, of course.' It was on that teaching course that Malcolm and I had met.

'And Anne got a research assistant's post in the university museum,' Malcolm said. 'Have I remembered right?'

'Yes,' I said.

'You know,' said Malcolm. 'Hearing you tell that story about Happy... I'd say, if I didn't know you better, married man and all, that you and Happy were a little bit in love. In fact, now I think about it, I wonder if Happy wasn't perhaps very much in love with you. You didn't seem to be responding... And that's what his problem was.'

'Oh shit,' I said. 'Now that's given me something to feel bad about.' I was making out that that idea had never crossed my mind. But I was being disingenuous. The idea that Happy had been in love with me had crossed my mind from time to time. At bad moments. In the dark spaces of bad nights.

I heard Malcolm say, 'None of us are responsible for the actions of others. If other people fall for us, that's their problem, not ours.'

I was grateful for that. I remembered a line of – I think – John Donne's. *That I love thee is no concern of thine.* Malcolm had just, very kindly, put that the other way round.

I looked at my watch. 'Oh my God,' I said. 'It's one o'clock. I've been rambling and keeping you up.'

'Don't worry about it,' Malcolm said. 'It's been an interesting evening. We can always sleep on the train tomorrow.'

Meanwhile we now got ready to go to bed.

I dreamt of Happy. But this time it was different. My imagination had made a leap. Perhaps because I'd been talking about him, perhaps because Malcolm had said something neither I nor anyone else had, and that I'd never confronted. Those words of Malcolm – *you and Happy were a little bit in love* – must have bitten deep.

In my dream Happy and I were sharing an armchair, seated side by side. It was a tight squeeze. I was conscious of the side of him, shoulder, arm and hip, pressed hard against me. My leg was squashed up against his. I felt the warmth of him for the first time ever. In life we'd scarcely ever touched. A handshake, perhaps, or a mock punch, would have been the most.

Did he then touch my head? Rumple my hair, perhaps? I'm not sure, because I awoke at that point. Awoke in confusion and embarrassment because I found I was coming, and it was too late to do anything to stop it, coming all over my host's sheets. I found myself using my hand to help the last of my semen out.

I was not only wet, but mortified. Why had this had to happen on my first night in Malcolm's spare bed? I should have worn pyjamas, I thought ruefully, or gone to bed in underpants. But that wasn't the worst of it. I'd never dreamt in that way about a man or boy before. Now I'd just made myself wet while dreaming of a male friend who was dead. It was a deep and unpleasant shock.

It was only five o'clock. I went back to sleep and dozed a bit, then, when I heard the others stirring, I got up.

I had to come clean about it, make a joke of it, at breakfast. 'I'm awfully sorry, Malcolm,' I said, assuming a sheepish grinning look. 'But I've had a wet dream in your sheets.'

Malcolm laughed, and so did Henri. *'Tu as fait la carte de France, comme on dit,'* he said: *You've made the map of France, as they say.* While Malcolm said, 'Don't worry about it. That's what sheets are for. Dreaming about Happy, no doubt.'

'Good God!' I said. 'Why on earth do you say that?' But then a dreadful thing happened. I began to blush deeply, and I saw Malcolm clock it. I saw him realise that, even if quite by accident, he had hit the nail on the head. He was kind enough not to say any more on the subject. He said something about the coffee we were drinking instead.

SEVEN

The *Train de Grande Vitesse* was still a novelty. The showpiece of French engineering, it had been introduced just a few years previously and, running on a brand new track from the suburbs of Paris to those of Lyon, had brought the two cities to within two hours of each other. Like a thread yanked tight in the hem of a garment it had, at one stroke, changed for ever the shape and scale of France. Sold to the regions as the key to their own futures, the TGV was meant to break the centralising grip of Paris on the economic life of the country. In reality the opposite was happening. True, some centres of industry and population were shifting along its golden plateway but always in the direction of the capital, not away from it.

But none of this was in my thoughts as Malcolm and I boarded the flame-coloured train at the Gare de Lyon that brilliant morning in July. Few of the passengers were dressed for business; most wore the expression, half anxious, half excited, of people bent on escape. Escape from work, escape from the city, escape too, this particular morning – though the patriotic among them would never had admitted it publicly – from something else. For today was no ordinary July Tuesday. It was the Fourteenth. Malcolm (a foreigner and therefore exempt from patriotic qualms) was able to voice their unspoken guilty thoughts.

'I've been through three *Quatorzes* and, frankly, I've

had them up to here. *Ras – le – bol!* It's always the same. The same tanks, the same fly past. The parade, the salute and the cavalry falling off their horses like clockwork on the same tight turn. The streets are impassable and the shops shut. You see it better on the television.

'Even the fireworks – they're spectacular, I must admit – can only be seen properly if you've got a friend with a well-sited balcony. Then to finish with there's the Firemen's Balls to tide you over painlessly from the *Quatorze* to the morning after. They can be fun, I grant you.' He paused to signal the inevitable tag. 'That is, if firemen's balls are really what you're into.'

For all the generosity of Malcolm's invitation I'd inevitably had some reservations about going to Provence with him. Holidays were notorious slayers of friendships. And I had feared that twelve days in the company of such a flamboyantly homosexual personality might prove rather wearing.

A few passengers were still arguing over the numbers of their seats and invoking the phlegmatic ticket controllers as referees when the double-length train slipped from its berth as imperceptibly as any cruise liner. It glided past the end of the platform, out from the shade of the station's arching canopy and into the embracing sunshine: a slender orange compass needle seeking South.

The south. That was the attraction, of course. It was the idea of the south that now awoke in me the eager excitement with which children begin their holidays. I determined to cast from my mind any reservations or anxieties about spending twelve days in close proximity to a gay man. It crossed my mind for a moment that perhaps those anxieties had added an extra piquancy to the venture. I told myself they had not.

Purposefully, with no sense of hurry, the train threaded its way through leafy outskirts, following at first the windings of the Seine until, without signalling the fact by so much as a click, the new track branched away from the old. Three, two, one, announced trackside panels silently to the driver and anyone who happened to be looking out of the window; then the train, already fast by any ordinary standard, effortlessly doubled its speed: a cantering horse changing up to full gallop. There was no sensation of the urgency of a plane on its take-off run or the breathless haste of a car on a race track. Rather it was as if the landscape had changed its focus; the senses that experienced it and plotted its reality in relation to time had selected a different magnification. And so the rolling pastures of northern Burgundy were conjured up from the normally endless-seeming plains of the Ile de France in a mere ten minutes. Another thirty minutes and Burgundy itself was left far behind in the slipstream of the train, now in free fall down the face of France.

Van Gogh had made the same journey, of course, as Malcolm now reminded me, although at a less exhilarating speed.

I told him Happy had once said that van Gogh's whole life had been a journey from darkness to light, from the cold north to the warm south, from the clouds to the sun.

I remembered Happy showing me the picture of the Potato Eaters. It wasn't one of the bright Van Gogh prints that had 'dis-endarkened' his bedroom walls; Happy had had to delve into a book to show me a photo of it, all black, brown and sepia. 'Then came Paris,' Happy had said. 'Two years there. And finally, off to the south where...' He'd tailed off and allowed the pictures in his book to articulate the rest of it. Van Gogh's two years in Provence had crowned his career with their celebration on canvas of his discovery of the light.

Now I remembered something else. Happy had added, 'Not everyone who begins that journey gets there at all.' Perhaps it was the unbearable poignancy of that remark that had caused me to blank the memory of the paintings on Happy's walls until it was woken by the sight of Malcolm's picture-hung apartment.

Time-charmed castles came and went among the changing perspectives of the hills while the Beaujolais mountains bided their time in the hazy distance. At last, decelerating smoothly, the train emerged from the uplands and, on a track as steep and winding as a staircase, descended to where the town of Lyon lay draped over the surrounding hills like a vast and richly patterned carpet.

'Impressive, isn't it?' said Malcolm. It was his first

experience of the TGV too.

'Too right,' I said.

A few minutes later – 'Sunflowers!' said Malcolm suddenly.

We had left behind the enormous spread of Lyon and were following the Rhone on its tortuous course down the valley that had linked the south of Europe with the north since prehistoric times. On the right now ran the broad river and on the left a field of yellow faces stared at the sun. Sunflowers.

'How much did that sunflower painting fetch, back in the spring?' Malcolm asked. 'The one they sold to a Japanese guy in London?'

'A lot,' I said. 'I don't remember how much.'

'Permit me to interrupt,' said a neighbour in heavily accented English. He was one of the few occupants of the carriage to wear a business suit. He was middle-aged, with shiny slicked-back hair and unusually lustrous dark eyes. He leaned forward to address us. 'I could not stop myself hearing. If it interests you it was twenty-two and a half million pounds sterling. A world record. Compare that, if you want, with the artist's poverty. Compare it even with mine.' He chuckled and gave us a business card that identified him as a fine art dealer from Arles. 'Pass and see me if you are in the town,' he said.

'Thank you,' we said.

Now town succeeded town, each vying for the brightest orange tiles, most luminous apricot walls and most brilliant blue sky. There was not a cloud to be seen by the time the profile of Mont Ventoux filled the eastern horizon and the train was coiling slowly round the ancient walls of Avignon, where the pennants atop the Palace of the Popes hung limply in the breathless afternoon. The air-conditioned train stopped and the door opened like an oven's. Our art dealing acquaintance gave us a discreet wave as we left the train while a tide of baking desert heat engulfed us when we stepped onto the platform.

Malcolm said, 'Which one of us do you reckon that guy fancied? The art dealer.'

It hadn't crossed my mind that he might have fancied either of us.

Despite the bustle of the season, we managed to find a hotel that suited our modest budgets and that first night it was so warm that we slept with all windows open and the shutters folded back. This suited me well since it helped to dispel the vague claustrophobia I'd imagined into existence at the prospect of sharing a room with Malcolm. In the event the experience was perfectly unthreatening – we undressed demurely with our backs to each other the way straight men do, and we then each donned a pair of pyjamas that (certainly my case, so quite probably also in Malcolm's) had not seen service in years, but had been hauled out of retirement precisely for the present unusual circumstances.

It was the first time I'd knowingly shared a bedroom with a gay man. Perhaps it was because of this that I had another wet dream in the middle of the night. This time I didn't know, when I awoke to find my hand a-flutter on my pulsing, spurting cock, what or who I had been dreaming about. That was just as well, I thought.

At least I didn't have to confess to Malcolm this time round. The sheets were not his but those of the Hotel Bristol. They were used to this, presumably, and semen stains – unless DNA testing is applied – are pretty anonymous.

But disaster had struck overnight, although in a very minor way. It came from a totally unexpected source: Malcolm and I both woke up studded with the largest and most painful mosquito bites we had ever experienced. We were sheepishly aware that we had been stupid not to foresee this. Three of the largest culprits could be clearly seen parked at dispersal stations around the walls; they were summarily squashed. Later we discovered the mosquito screens for the windows in the wardrobe.

'It's not as if they just itched,' Malcolm complained, applying a preparation we got from the pharmacy – at some expense. 'They remind you of their existence every few minutes with a little stab of pain. It's worse than wasps' stings.' We had agreed in advance that we'd come to relax, do some sightseeing, drive round the region following the Van Gogh trail, and eat drink and sleep a little more than usual. 'No sport,' Malcolm had insisted. 'At least, not for me. If you want to go out jogging on your own, that's just fine, and I'll hole up in some suitable bar while you do it – unless it's at sparrows' fart in which case I'll simply stay in bed. And if you want to play a game of cricket and can find another twenty-one people with the same inclination, then that's fine by me too. Only don't ask me to be the referee or whatever it is you call it. For snooker, though, or pétanque – well, I'm up for those if you find you get a craving.' Holidaying with friends was all about compromises. I thought I could live with this one.

EIGHT

We spent our first day wandering in the ancient squares and alleys of Avignon and in the evening we dined in the coolest spot in town: an old lane with a stream flowing beside it. It boasted a small restaurant housed in what appeared to be an antique shop. There was only one dish on the menu, a *daube* of wild boar, and only one wine, a local red, served in engraved goblets. We ate with just six other diners, all at the same table, surrounded by leather-bound books and gilt-framed mirrors that reflected the candle-light, and surveyed by a statue of Saint Lucy, who carried her own eyes before her on a dish like two poached eggs. The proprietors – he the waiter, she the cook – kept watch on us customers from across the street, sitting in the cool on the low wall that divided river from road. The bill when it came was modest in relation to the quality of the experience.

Someone had told us of a garage in Avignon that rented out cars at a third of the normal price, and the nest day we sought it out. It had been decided that Malcolm, veteran of French roads, would do most of the driving and I could make my debut, if I wanted to, in some anonymous rural spot. But this plan had to be drastically rethought when Malcolm discovered that his driving licence remained in Paris. So I received my initiation into the ways of most of the motoring world among the morning traffic on the six lanes of the Avignon ring road. The car was neither new nor pretty – not that those things bothered us. More disturbing was the rear-view mirror's habit of sliding down the windscreen like a snail in fast motion.

Never mind. The sun was hot and we were high on the effects of our surroundings: colour, scent and countryside; escape from Paris, in Malcolm's case and, in mine, escape from just about everything else.

The road took us that morning to the hilltop village of Gordes where we could afford nothing except the view, and then to the shaded valley of Sénanques where a timeless Cistercian abbey rode like a ship at anchor on a bee-buzzing lavender sea. Then the mid-day sun swept into the valley like a blow-torch. 'Want to visit somewhere cooler?' Malcolm asked.

We found the canyon of Fontaine de Vaucluse. At the narrow head of the valley green waters welled from a cave so deep that not even Cousteau had got to the bottom of it and here, centuries before, Petrarch had settled reclusively to contemplate the beauties of nature and his absent Laura. The sky at this point was reduced to a narrow blue ribbon across which kites sailed from time to time, going from one horizon to the other in half a dozen seconds. A little lower down the gorge the sky broadened out with the river. Here white-bibbed dippers plunged and darted in the icy waters that, unable to agree upon their own level, argued noisily among the rocks.

Malcolm found a smooth slab of rock that seemed to have been placed deliberately in midstream for the convenience of sunbathers and, hopping across to it, installed himself there. He was not born to be a sunbather as I could see from his reddening knees and nose but, in adopting the attitude of one, he looked as comfortable and relaxed as I, now perched on a boulder nearby, could remember seeing him. His face had lost its habitual tension and his eyes, which I had always thought of as black, now seemed no darker than hazel as they caught the reflection of the brightness above.

'What do you want to be when you grow up?' Malcolm called across to me. It was an unexpected question.

'Be?' I asked. 'Or do?' I felt happier, lighter, than I'd done for weeks. Was it Malcolm's company that had done that?

'Either. Both,' Malcolm said laughingly. 'Doesn't matter – though I appreciate the distinction.'

'I actually thought I was grown-up already. Don't you think that at twenty-eight – and you ought to be an authority now that you're twenty-eight as well – I should be?'

'Should be, perhaps. Yes, at twenty-eight you should be.' There was an unspoken reservation in Malcolm's answer. I let it go without challenging. Between my boulder and Malcolm's rock slab gushed a torrent of water a metre wide, though the noise and urgency of its progress made it seem broader than that.

'I once thought I'd grown up,' Malcolm continued, as much to himself as to me. 'Then I found I hadn't. And now...' The phrase tailed off in the splashing of the water. He turned towards me. 'How would you like to live here?'

'What? Like Petrarch? A solitary hermit in a hut? 'The world forgetting, by the world forgot.' I'm not sure I would. It is a bit extreme down here in this chasm. Winter evenings might get a bit depressing, I imagine.'

'Well all right, not precisely here maybe. But in Provence. Or anywhere in *la France Profonde*.'

'What?'

Malcolm was speaking quietly and the rushing water was very loud.

'*La France Profonde*. Deepest France. I would.'

'Would what?'

'Like to live here.'

This surprised me. 'I always thought you were a town mouse.'

'Appearances are defective, as someone probably said already or ought to have done. I was born in the wilds of Cornwall. I must have told you that. The wilds of Provence would be quite like home – if a bit warmer. But then I'm at home everywhere. And nowhere too, of course. And you?'

'And me what?' I wasn't sure if I'd caught all the words. It would be easier without the rapids between us.

'Would you like to live in Provence?' Malcolm articulated the question and at the same moment I rose from my rocky perch and leaped across the stream. I landed neatly astride Malcolm's waist but then nearly toppled backwards into the current. To steady myself I dropped to a crouching position and accidentally found myself kneeling astride him and grasping his shoulders.

Malcolm gave me a smile of surprise. At that precise moment I found it appealing and boyish.

'That's better,' I said. 'Now I can hear you properly.' I laughed; I wasn't quite sure why. Perhaps it was the unexpected novelty of my position, almost sitting on top of Malcolm and peering into his face. The novelty of seeing Malcolm smiling up at me like that, his smile almost turning to a laugh. I said, 'Yes, perhaps I wouldn't mind living in Provence, though I'd want to see a bit more of it first. And it would depend who with, of course. What were you trying to say about being at home everywhere?'

'And nowhere,' Malcolm answered seamlessly. 'And by the same token. Like the wandering Jew, as Verlaine said in a poem called *Walcourt* – which you should read if you haven't already. Only Verlaine wasn't Jewish. I mean, not literally.' He looked straight up into my eyes. 'And neither are we.'

And then for some reason which I'm still not able to explain properly, I leaned down and kissed Malcolm on the lips. It was an equal surprise for both of us.

A second later I detached himself from Malcolm and rolled a short distance across the rock slab. I felt confused and awkward, though nothing worse than that. 'Have you got a cigarette?' I asked.

NINE

There were no wet dreams that night. Not for me at any rate. As for Malcolm, well, I didn't ask. There are some things you don't.

Another of those things you don't ask friends, but wait till they volunteer the information, is the question, *Why did you get divorced?* Another, *Whose fault was it?* Malcolm hadn't asked me anything about my divorce, and I'd volunteered very little to date. To my surprise I found myself wanting to answer those unasked questions of his when I awoke the next morning, even though I knew I'd find the subject difficult. I wondered if this had something to do with the extraordinary fact that I'd given him a kiss.

The heat was quite something. We decided to move to L'Isle sur la Sorgue, a small and slumberous town whose name's every syllable suggested the plash of water wheels and encircling streams. It was about an hour's drive from Avignon, and when we arrived we found it looking every bit as lovely as the sound of its name. There were the water wheels, there were the streams. As we whiled away the end of the afternoon on one of its old plane-shaded terraces, dragonflies skimmed up and down the watercourse beside us, their reds, greens and blues providing a changing pattern of jewels against the backcloth of the jade-green crowfoot whose tresses seemed almost to fill the fast-flowing river. One dragonfly landed on Malcolm's wristwatch and stared with its shiny Martian face uncomprehendingly at the passing time.

'Only the big ones are really dragonflies,' I said. 'The little ones are damsel-flies.'

'Call them what you like, they're both beautiful,' Malcolm said.

A battered Renault Four pulled up alongside us. It was white, with a rainbow transfer applied along the side. It also had more than the usual number of dents and craters. It had been rammed from the rear, attacked frontally and subjected to the odd broadside as well. 'I bet that comes from Paris,' Malcolm said.

Out of the Renault stepped a young woman, blonde, slender, who turned her face away from us just at the moment when I realised that it was beautiful. Moving with the grace of a dancer, transforming her simple dress by the way she wore it, she crossed the road and disappeared into a shop.

'Now that,' I said, 'is the eternal feminine of France.' I realised I was rather waving my heterosexual credentials in Malcolm's face. Perhaps I needed to do that though, after yesterday's kiss.

'Her background?' Malcolm asked. This was a game we'd used to play when we were together learning to teach, though we hadn't done since.

'Ballet teacher,' I suggested. 'Or masseuse.'

'Nothing so physical,' Malcolm said. 'She does wonderful things for the poor in the third world. She's a plain-clothes nun.'

When she came out of the shop she was encumbered with an enormous though not heavy-looking parcel ('knitted blankets for Bangladesh,' said Malcolm) that got in her way when she came to unlock her car. I was sitting only inches away. I sprang up and took the parcel from her while she dealt with the door. I was rewarded with a bright though brief smile and a *merci beaucoup*. Then she drove away.

'Thus,' said Malcolm, 'does the beautiful dragonfly emerge from its chrysalis, even as from a beat-up Renault, and disappear for ever into the wide blue.'

'The damsel-fly as well,' I said. 'And which was she, do you suppose?'

'A damsel or a dragon?' Malcolm queried. 'Let's say a damsel, shall we? Be nice and give her the benefit of the doubt?'

We were returning later that evening from a substantial restaurant meal when Malcolm came to a halt in the middle of a small square and exclaimed: 'Good God! Look at that.'

'At what?' I said

'That café. The Café de France. It's a dead-ringer for the *Terrasse du Café le Soir*. Look. The light spilling out on the pavement, the round tables, the awning – even the dark street beyond with its lighted windows, even the stars above.'

'Was this the very place, perhaps?' I asked.

'No,' said Malcolm authoritatively. 'Vincent painted a café in Arles. But he got the actual idea for the picture from a description in Guy de Maupassant.'

'Of the same café?'

'No such luck. De Maupassant was describing a boulevard café in Paris. Which just goes to show how we go round in circles. Nothing is what it seems or where you expect to find it. And when you begin a journey the destination is never the one you thought you were setting out for.' Malcolm paused for a second. 'Look, we're in a direct line for home now. Reckon to call in for a route-map on the way?' A route-map was a new coinage of Malcolm's own: an alloy of night-cap and one for the road. I found I was up for that.

And so we walked up from the square onto the lighted café terrace. It was as if we were actually walking into Vincent's bright canvas. I felt a frisson among the hairs at the back of my neck.

'Hey!' Malcolm said when we were installed at one of the terrace tables among the beau monde of L'Isle sur la Sorgue. 'It's the dragonfly.'

'Damsel-fly, didn't we agree?' I prompted.

'As you want.'

The damsel, or dragon, was sitting at the next table with two other young people, one of each sex, who were clearly a couple. After a moment she nodded across in recognition and after a few more seconds Malcolm asked her if he and I could join their table, something which I, had I been alone, would not have thought of doing. Well, I might have thought of it. But only thought.

As Malcolm had said, appearances were defective. The damsel was a journalist who worked for the *Dépêche du Midi* and her friends were, respectively, a nuclear physicist and an infant school teacher. The man taught in infant school, his girlfriend wore the white coat.

The first route-map begged a second and once the internationality as well as the francophone credentials of the gathering had been established, conversation developed on a number of subjects which the world was at that time waiting to have put right.

The waiter arrived to chat and to elicit a further order. Malcolm took advantage of the ensuing buzz to say to me in English, 'You could make that woman tonight if you wanted.'

For some reason I found myself appalled by his suggestion. 'Are you joking?' I hissed.

'Only partly,' Malcolm said. 'I know you won't, of

course. But if you wanted to. The couple will go in a few minutes, I can sense it. She'll stay to see what will happen. Two minutes later I plead a headache and retire. The rest is up to you. I'll keep the room warm till you get back. If you do get back before breakfast time, throw stones at the window.'

I was even more appalled at hearing this eminently practical scenario spelled out so simply, so clinically. 'Get away,' I whispered.

Another route-map was agreed and ordered. One or two more conversational hares were started only to be lost sight of in the shimmer of the summer night. The glasses empty, the three French people took their leave together.

'Guess your vibes weren't all that positive,' concluded Malcolm.

I felt an explanation was necessary. 'It's just that casual sex doesn't hold a great deal of attraction for me at the moment. Perhaps it never has done. I can't explain. Perhaps...'

The waiter arrived to offer us a drink on behalf of the *patron* – a traditional form of long-service medal. After that it seemed necessary for some reason to buy one back for the patron and another for the waiter. As Malcolm had said, we were on a straight line for home.

Malcolm leaned across the table towards me. 'We still have time to talk, don't we?' he said smoothly. That is, if you have anything you specially want to talk about.'

Was the guy a mind-reader? 'Yes,' I said. 'Funny you should say that. There is.'

'Thought there might be,' Malcolm said.

TEN

Here we were, on the terrace of a café that looked uncannily like the one that Van Gogh had made world famous, and Malcolm had invited me to talk. It was the moment I'd been waiting for all that day – perhaps for longer. It was a moment, under the fading evening sky, with a friend, over a drink, that was made for opening up. 'I told you I didn't like Beethoven,' I heard myself suddenly, erratically, begin. 'And that Happy told me I'd one day come to change my mind. Well, I did change my mind a few years later. I'd like to tell you about the person who carried out the conversion. I was a Schubert freak at that time. You may remember that.' Malcolm nodded. 'Happy used to quote a famous musician who said, 'Schubert is a forest in sunshine and shadow; Beethoven a mountain range.''

'Uh-huh,' said Malcolm, making an effort to follow this. 'So who showed you the mountains?'

'I'm going to tell you,' I said. 'I didn't exactly choose to become a school teacher,' I continued. 'But what else did you do with an English degree? I was just about to get married. People started to talk about security and so on and before long, so did I. The training course beckoned. It pointed towards a life of school, of marriage and family, with long summer holidays on the plus side and late nights marking essays on the minus.'

'It was the same for me,' Malcolm reminded me. 'The

same for all of us.'

'Sorry,' I said. 'You went through the training course with me. I haven't forgotten that. It's just that we haven't seen much of each other since, and I've never really told you what happened after that.' Malcolm nodded. I pressed on. 'My first year as a teacher went really well. I'd got a job just outside Durham which was lucky. You did know that, of course. Anne was still there doing research and we'd managed to rent a house really cheaply on the edge of town. The headmaster thought I was doing a good job as beginners go, that I was energetic – for that read young and naïf – and I managed all right with discipline. Don't ask me how. Most of the kids even seemed to like me.'

'Why do you sound so surprised?' asked Malcolm.

I ignored that. Now I'd started, there seemed an awful lot I wanted to get out. 'After a year or so I started to panic. About work I mean. About the results of it all.'

'I don't get you. Exam results?'

'No, of course not. I mean the real results. The results of my teaching those kids the language of Shakespeare, Wilde, Lawrence...'

'And what was the result?'

'Nearly non-existent. Or so it seemed to me for the best part of two years. Naturally I talked to my colleagues about it and they did their best to be positive. They suggested for instance that just by keeping them busy in the classroom, Shakespeare and I were stopping the kids from vandalising phone boxes and stealing motor bikes. I didn't think a great deal of that argument. It didn't make me feel any better for one thing and it didn't reflect too well on poor old Shakespeare either.'

'Oh, I don't know. Anyone from the seventeenth century who can save modern phone boxes from vandals can't be all bad. Don't forget, I've been a school teacher myself.'

'Of course,' I said I was talking as if I hadn't remembered that. It was the drink, of course. 'Sorry.' But I went on anyway.

'I was saying I didn't have any discipline problems. Well, that was almost entirely true. There was one kid though, just one in all the classes I taught, who was a perfect pest. He was fourteen when I arrived at the school, very bright but younger than the rest of his class and a late physical developer into the bargain. He made up for this by being an attention-seeker, irritatingly trying to be witty in class. His classmates found him witty, of course, his teachers just irritating. Me included. If there was a double entendre to be dredged up out of a text he was always the one to find it and then question me about it with an insolently straight face. Then he'd dream up the kind of classroom pranks the others had grown out of years before – you know, alarm clocks going off in locked cupboards, gerbils in the waste-paper basket, that sort of thing...' Malcolm nodded. He knew only too well, of course.

'Well, you get the picture. This kid was called Ian Lewis. There's an Ian in every school; you also know that. They're nice as anything outside the classroom. They just go mental inside it. And they're quite impervious to punishment. Ian was once actually thrown out of a detention class for being disruptive.'

'I'm beginning to like this kid,' said Malcolm. 'Go on.'

'For some reason I found it doubly infuriating because he was good at English and also he read better than the others – at least he could once he forgot about sending the text sky high. One day – by now he was about sixteen and had already been a pain in the arse for two years – we were doing King Lear and I'd asked him to read the part of the King. He came to the line, 'And my poor fool is hanged', where he suddenly stopped and couldn't go on. I looked at him a bit apprehensively, wondering what we were in for, expecting some kind of joke I suppose. But what I saw surprised me much more: his face was running with tears. Why that particular line had moved him I don't know. There are others more obviously pathetic. Maybe, simply, the whole tragedy had come home to him all at once in that single moment. Now it went through my head that I had the perfect opportunity to humiliate him in front of his classmates and put an end to his two years of attempted sabotage in a split second. Some teachers would have done.'

Malcolm said grimly, 'I've known a few who did.'

I said, 'The fact I even thought about it just shows

how much he'd tried everyone. But I didn't make a conscious decision. I simply finished the line myself and read the part of the king till the end of the scene. A few of the kids looked at me, surprised, but nobody looked at him and he was able to recover himself without losing face. Men still weren't allowed to cry in the north-east of England and certainly not when only sixteen.

'Neither of us referred to the incident at the time by even so much as a smile but the change in his behaviour could hardly have been more remarkable – at least in my classes. I say that because I gathered from other teachers that with them he went on pretty much as before, but I never had any trouble from him again. He still liked to lark about, but the destructive thing seemed to have evaporated.'

I took a slurp of wine. 'From that day on I started to enjoy teaching once again. Quite suddenly, quite immediately. And though this was less immediate, the kid began to talk to me outside the classroom, just in the ordinary way. It was something the others all did as a matter of course but, before then, he didn't. He took to button-holing me after lessons with questions about literature, then later with chit-chat about life in general. I began to lend him books I thought would interest him. Then he found his way to our house. Of course he met Anne. Time passed and we all became – well, friends, I suppose. Though with me there was always that space, that fire-break that has to exist between a teacher and a … a non-adult pupil. I got invited to his house. I met his parents and his sister. Becoming a sort of confidant, if you like, I got treated to his views on everything from euthanasia to socialism.'

'And were they earth-shaking?'

'No.' I laughed at the memory. 'But his musical tastes... Well, I mentioned Beethoven. I once said flippantly to Ian that Schubert was worth ten Beethovens. That was a hornets' nest all right. The boy had just had a road to Damascus experience on hearing a disc of some of the piano sonatas played by Artur Schnabel.'

'Who?'

'First person to record all Beethoven's piano music, back in the thirties. Ian had been collecting all the discs one by one. So I was subjected to them, listening grudgingly. But little by little I was converted in my turn. Not just to Schnabel but to Beethoven too – as Happy predicted.'

'After music, the theatre. Anne and I began taking Ian with us to plays in Newcastle occasionally, and sometimes to the cinema. He moved very easily between his own family and us. When the summer came we'd go walking, sometimes the three of us, sometimes Ian and me, sometimes Ian and Anne. It was a beautiful summer, just before Ian began his last year at school, and perhaps the beauty of it blinded me to other things that should have been obvious.'

Malcolm said, incredulously, 'You're not going to tell me he seduced your wife?'

'No, nothing like that. Well, not really. In the autumn he was going to do the Oxbridge entrance exams. He had to have special classes in English, obviously. That meant me. Sometimes at the school, sometimes at his parents' home, or at ours. A bit irregular, I suppose, but we were all family and friends by now.

'One Saturday morning in November when Anne had gone to visit her parents for the weekend I got a phone-call, quite late, from Ian. He was on his own, he said, and was feeling nervous about his Oxford interview. Would I be able to come over for a chat? I said that I could. By that stage the request seemed quite natural and if I sensed something strangely agitated in his voice I'd have put it down to his exam nerves.

'When I got there he was more than nervous. Not exactly drunk, though he'd obviously been to the pub earlier. And I did think it odd when he announced that he'd been left alone in the house for the entire weekend. He explained that his parents thought his sister was at home and his sister thought his parents were. OK, he was seventeen by now and well able to take care of himself but his parents were the careful sort, over-protective if anything, and the last people to leave a teenager alone for the weekend by mistake. I asked him how it had come about. He just grinned and said, "I fixed it." Then he offered me a glass of his father's malt whisky.'

'Which you refused like a good boy?'

'At first, yes. But Ian launched into a crazy spiel

about me and him which I couldn't – or just didn't want to – understand. It wasn't till he threw himself into his father's armchair and said in so many words that it was time he told me he loved me that it really sank in. At first I just gaped at him. He repeated what he'd said. 'It's time I told you I love you.' Then I found I wanted that drink. As I poured it I saw – like drowning people who see their lives pass before them – images whose significance seemed to have been hidden from me till then. I can't explain how. I saw Ian smiling at me from his classroom desk, not just once but on dozens of occasions over the years. Smiles which had meant nothing at the time but which now seemed to engage like gears to drive a whole engine of realisation. Now I saw him, only three months earlier, on one of our walks, slipping out of his clothes and plunging into the River Wear; only now did I see how deliberately he had done it, how he had made sure I was looking. There were other occasions... I was seeing in one moment what I'd failed to see in four years.'

A bat fluttered low over our heads under the awning before swooping up under the street-lamp in pursuit of some invisible insect. 'Go on,' said Malcolm.

'Hindsight is wonderful. It tells me now, as it no doubt tells you, that for my own safety I should have left the house there and then. I can see you're thinking that not many people would believe the story I've just told you. Well you're right. Not many people did. I'll come to that. But at the time I didn't sense any danger. Stupidly I imagined that because I didn't reciprocate his feelings I wasn't compromised by staying where I was. Huh! I used to think queer schoolmasters who got into that kind of situation had only themselves to blame when their careers collapsed in scandal and acrimony. Well, I was right of course, but not necessarily for the reason I used to imagine. OK, I stayed, and I'm to blame for that. I tried at first to persuade him he was mistaken. I suggested he had drunk too much, that he was nervous, excited, going through an adolescent phase... Anything. I thought I was being helpful. I soon realised. My words only enraged him. He searched around for the worst insult he could throw at me. "Typical fucking grown-up" was what he came up with. Before long we were shouting at each other all over the house. I'd stopped trying to be reasonable. I was furious with him for putting me in a position that was getting more desperate by the minute. The discussion was now way out of my control; I didn't know how or when it would end.

'Finally he collapsed in tears, howling, on his bed. That was another cue for my exit and this time I decided to take it. I touched him gently on the shoulder, meaning simply, "Goodnight and no hard feelings." He turned, grabbed me, caught me off balance and quickly pulled me down on top of him. He made a move, as I thought, to kiss me. Only he didn't. He sank his teeth into my neck. I yelled as much with surprise as pain – and in that moment the door opened and his parents walked in. Their plans had changed for some reason. You won't be surprised to know that I no longer remember what the reason was.' I stopped speaking and looked up. Malcolm's face was expressionless. I couldn't guess what he was thinking. I resumed,

'I'll skip the next few minutes if you don't mind. It makes me wince even now, though the days and weeks that followed were nearly as bad. Before eight o'clock the next morning – Sunday, remember – I'd had a phone-call from the headmaster. He suggested I might like to take the following week as a paid holiday and call on him for a drink on the Monday. When I did call, he was surprisingly sympathetic. He gave me a cheque for the next term's salary in lieu of notice and explained that this was necessary since Ian's parents were considering taking proceedings against both myself and the school. He reassured me that it was all talk and nothing would come of it but said it would help everyone concerned if I promised never to contact Ian again. He even had a typed document for me to sign, making the undertaking concrete. He also told me that it would be unwise of me to apply for a school-teaching post again. News travelled fast, he said, and the kindest reference he could give me would never be kind enough. He said he'd further my search for any other kind of employment in any way he could. He couldn't speak too highly of my gifts or of my services to the school. He regretted losing me deeply. It was all one of those dreadful things that happen in life. The awful thing was that he meant every word. He was quite unprepared to discuss what had happened and silenced me with his hand when I tried to speak. It appeared that my own guilt or innocence was a total irrelevance. He gave me three large gins during all this. God, I needed them. I was growing up quickly that week.'

'But you signed that paper without a fight?' Malcolm said in a tone of near disbelief. 'You didn't have to do that. If you were as guiltless as you say – and I don't have to tell you that I believe that – you could have proved it, with testimony from Ian, in a court. Innocent until proven guilty. Or did the boy put the boot in?'

'No he didn't. Anne did.'

'Oh bloody hell. How come? And why?'

'That was the worst thing. I phoned her, naturally, as soon as I got home, panicking, that Saturday night. But something in her tone made me uneasy and when she arrived the next day it became more and more apparent that she – of all people – didn't believe my version of events. It was incredible. I was lost. Not only did she disbelieve me, she minded desperately. She persuaded herself somehow that she had always had misgivings about my relationship with Ian, that she had always thought – 'subconsciously' was the word she used – that I might be homosexual and had stifled the thought for years. Can you imagine? Your own wife tells you something like that! You know it to be untrue but…' I looked at Malcolm, challenging him to disagree with this, but he said nothing. I relaxed slightly and went on. 'Well, without Anne's backing I felt unable to defend myself somehow; it was as if the foundations had shifted, and I just collapsed. I signed the bloody paper and was deprived at a stroke of my job, Ian's company, and, eventually, Anne's too.'

'She divorced you.'

'As soon as she could. Since she felt so strongly I suppose she had to. But why feel so strongly about something so mistaken, so untrue? That's what I still can't get over, still find hard to take.'

Malcolm nodded slowly, sympathetically. 'It still hurts, of course. I understand that. What happened to Ian?'

'He was very shaken up for a bit. Was even ill for a time. Messed up his Oxbridge exam. Still, he got over it soon enough as youngsters do. Did all right when it came to A-levels and got a university place at London.'

'So you've seen him since?'

'No, certainly not. I heard that by chance from one of his ex-classmates I bumped into. And that's all I heard.'

'Gosh,' said Malcolm soberly, although sober was a long way from describing his state.

'I've probably told you too much,' I said, suddenly conscious of how much I'd said.

'Actually,' Malcolm said, 'you probably haven't told me enough. Though probably just about enough for tonight. It'll take me a while to get my head round that. Perhaps it's time we headed back.' With a bit of difficulty we got to our feet, thanked the waiter, who was putting the chairs on the tables – on every table except ours, that is – and said *Bonne nuit.*

ELEVEN

The hotel had provided us with a key to the street door in the event of a late return. That was fortunate. It was nearly two o'clock. But we couldn't make the key fit the only lock. I tried, then Malcolm tried, then we both tried, struggling as much against each other as with the key. But it was not a question eventually of the key's needing a knack to turn it. The key was simply too big to enter the slot at all. We knocked. Loudly and often. No answer came. 'There must be another door,' said Malcolm. There was. We found it with some effort about three yards from the first. This one was a hundred or more years older, a confection of gnarled oak boards and iron studs. Its key-hole was of Jack and the Beanstalk proportions. Our little modern key could poke about in it for ever and not touch the sides.

A black shadow now in an even blacker street, the hotel became a medieval fortress and we were without the means to capture it by night. The town was silent now except for the steady spurt of water through old mill paddles. Drunkenly we cursed our luck, the hotel, the town and everyone in it. Then I noticed a crack of light at the join of a pair of shutters on the top floor. I shouted up to it – something I wouldn't have done at such an hour when sober; perhaps the climate had something to do with it – *'Holà, holà,'* though that was the wrong language, and was agreeably amazed when, after a few repetitions, the shutters were flung open. Yellow light spilled out, bright and warm against the cobalt night. A silhouette was framed in the opening.

'Qu'est-ce qu'il y a?' called an Italian-accented male voice.

'Can you let us in?'

'Didn't they give you a key?'

'It's the wrong one. It doesn't work,' said Malcolm.

'Are you drunk?'

'Not specially,' said Malcolm, his injured tone indicating, why do you ask?

'Wait. I'm coming down.' The window emptied.

The door was opened easily from the inside and a smiling, suntanned young man stood before us. The suntan was more remarkable than the smile because it stretched from head to toe without the interruption of the smallest stitch of clothing. He chuckled and, forming his hand into a fist, applied it to his nose with a rotating gesture, as if attaching a false one. 'Drunk?' he repeated the question. 'Upstairs we're all drunk.' He shrugged. I hadn't realised before that a shrug involved all the muscles from the thighs up. The discovery fascinated me. 'And now you too? That's as it should be,' said the Italian, at that moment showing the first signs of an erection.

Malcolm seemed to have lost the power of speech. It was left to me to murmur, *'Merci,'* and to the Italian to point out the small keyhole we had overlooked among the crevices of the oaken door while we were focused, each of us with one eye shut, on trying to make our key fit the larger one.

'Sleep well,' said the Italian and then paused, perhaps to choose the goodnight gesture that most fitted the situation. In the end he rumpled the hair on top of both our heads – one hand each – and pattered quickly upstairs. By the time we had recovered our wits he was out of sight

Malcolm's friend Peter had talked of having a Van Gogh window opposite his flat in Paris. It shouldn't have been surprising to find another one turning up here on what was pretty much Vincent's home patch. It was more surprising to find this one harbouring neither damsel nor dragon but a flesh and blood, naked, Italian male with the body of a Renaissance athlete and not a fig leaf in sight. But, drunk as I was, I was hardly surprised by what happened next.

Malcolm was all over me before we had even got up the stairs, and my brief kiss of yesterday afternoon was being returned with a quite phenomenal accumulation of interest. And I, drunk as I was, found myself returning Malcolm's kisses quite fulsomely, despite the faint promptings of my more sober self that I didn't really want this, it was sure to lead to complications, and I'd be sorry in the morning. Once inside our room though, we were both out of our clothes in no time, fully aroused and rolling in each other's arms, on one of the beds – it had not yet been decided which was whose, and right now the question would hardly have had meaning. But then, just as Malcolm's hand began to get to grips with my dick and mine drunkenly with his, something happened. It was as if a switch had been thrown somewhere among the circuits of my dulled consciousness, and I heard myself say, 'Sorry, Malcolm. This isn't for us.' With a bit of an effort I extricated myself from Malcolm's embracing arms and legs – the effort being necessary not because Malcolm put up that much of a struggle, but because I was having difficulty co-ordinating my own movements. Then I stumbled off to the bathroom, finding that I quite genuinely needed to pee. When I returned, Malcolm was conclusively tucked up in one of the beds and not looking at me, though he did say, quite civilly, 'I guess that wasn't too good an idea after all.'

'OK,' I said. 'Let's forget it, shall we? Go to sleep now?'

We did. We slept like rocks and woke up with very bad headaches. We were too late for breakfast at the hotel and had to scour the town for coffee and croissants in the middle of the morning. We were not surprised to find the Italian, now fully clothed and with a group of friends, doing the same thing. We greeted each other with warm smiles of recognition, shaking hands among the café tables and exchanging a few hackneyed words about hangovers. We all said *tu* to one another as though the singularity of the previous night's encounter automatically licensed this familiarity. But, breakfast over, we never saw the Italian again.

We didn't discuss the embarrassing bedtime episode. We became talkative and bright after breakfast – an astute witness might have said too bright. It seemed we had both decided to declare the incident null and void.

Malcolm suggested St-Rémy as our next destination, I said: 'Why not?' I'd never heard of the place and would have said the same to San Sebastian or St Moritz. Despite my swimming head, this was the day I found the car becoming less of a problem. For the first time I began to feel it quite natural that oncoming traffic should hurl itself towards me on my left instead of approaching politely from the right as it did in England. It no longer startled me that the gear-lever should leave its knob in my hand whenever I needed to change down particularly suddenly. Even the fact that the car tended to weave from side to side at speeds of over a hundred kilometres per hour no longer bothered me; no more did the violent vibration that started up simultaneously in the steering column.

By the time we arrived in St-Rémy I had learned, thanks to Malcolm, that this was the place where Van Gogh had spent the second of his two Provence years. But I suspected that the town was important to Malcolm for some reason more personal than this.

A circlet of miniature boulevards lined with plane trees protected the tiny town centre like a charm. Once on the inside there was little place for traffic or its emissions, and no room for troubled thoughts; those things were left behind like wild dogs outside the stockade of plane trees.

Van Gogh was in evidence everywhere. The sites he had chosen to paint were drawn to the attention of visitors by discreetly placed reproductions. He had not actually lived in the charmed town centre but a little way outside it – in the insane asylum, to be brutally precise. That might have been expected to put a damper on his appreciation of the place. But the pictures that I saw all around me seemed blessedly infected with the sunny, extrovert charms of the town. Charms that had begun to work on me as soon as I arrived, dispelling troubling thoughts.

Not only Van Gogh but also Nostradamus had lived in this place. Nostradamus who had dared to reveal a fearsome future to a God-fearing past. I said, 'It's hard to imagine anyone having such terrifying visions in so placid a spot.'

Malcolm answered by showing me a Van Gogh picture. It only took a minute to find a copy of it on a postcard outside a shop. In it the painter had depicted St-Rémy as if snugly tucked up for the night, in bed among the soft enfolding hills. A few lights glowed complacently from the cheerful houses that nestled around the church spire in the centre. But the sleepy town was blissfully unaware of the celestial high-jinks in progress above. A vast crescent moon seemed to be trying to touch its toes in a radiant furnace of energy while stars and constellations exploded in Catherine wheels of sparks. The Milky Way itself rolled like phosphorescent ocean waves and broke in glittering showers on distant hills.

'The heavens at play while mankind sleeps?' Malcolm hazarded. 'There's Nostradamus in context for you, if you want. Does it help you to make sense of things, do you think?'

I chose not to ask him what things he thought I was trying to make sense of. I'd realised that I knew that picture very well. It had had pride of place on Happy's wall all those years ago. Was that the terrifying night sky he had gone out to look for on his lonely winter walks? Was it the one he had finally found on the last one?

Malcolm must have noticed my moment of silent thoughtfulness. He said, 'Ghosts of yours in the picture?' But I didn't answer, and he didn't press me. Not then.

TWELVE

We drove out of the town past the asylum and up into the Alpilles, the cockscomb of mini-mountains between St-Rémy and the sea. From here we could see the whole Rhone delta, from Montpelier to Marseille, the distant sweep of the Mediterranean shimmering beyond its inlets and lagoons. Inland lay Avignon, asleep like a tawny beast in its loop of the Rhone, while over to the east the wispy outlines of Alpine peaks emerged and vanished by turn like summer clouds amidst the haze.

The heat was intense, energy-sapping; all life was invested in the light, the colour and the scents around. Winding down from the hills on our return to St-Rémy, we passed the ruins of a Roman town not long since resurrected from encroaching olive groves. Here we sat out the hottest part of the day in the shade of a dark green cypress tree. Actually we didn't sit. We lay on our backs on the grass. In order to stay in the shade we had to move round it in circular fashion as time went on, like the two hands of a clock. Redstarts and wheatears flitted among the ancient stones, feeding in the forum, nesting in the recesses of the baths, unaffected by the heat. The air was vibrant with the rattle of cicadas and – when anything moved to disturb them – it shimmered with their wings. A few yards away a praying mantis crouched at its devotions while a procession of ants made their penitential way across the hot stones, engaged in some alternative ritual of their own. Beyond the excavations stretched cornfields too bright for comfort, their blazing yellow not relieved but only intensified by the red of their scatter of poppies. At their edge the rooftops of the asylum rose from the valley and beyond them the needle-sharp spire of St-Rémy itself. On the other side the saw-toothed outline of the Alpilles was shaded in with blue and mauve. It all looked oddly familiar.

A thought slowly took shape in my mind. Eventually I said: 'It isn't the first time you've sat under this tree, is it?' Where the thought had come from I never knew.

Malcolm smiled. 'No. I came here with a previous boyfriend.'

'Called?' I asked.

'Aidan.'

'I don't remember…'

'I might not have told you. It was during the years when we weren't in contact very much. I thought it was going to last for ever with Aidan. We came to France together, wandering Jews. By the time we found this spot – we're where Vincent painted Les Blés Jaunes, you may have realised – we'd been lovers for two years.'

I said, 'Not bad for a gay relationship.' At once I saw what an insensitive thing I'd said. Malcolm was kind enough to take no notice. He went on.

'Aidan was the Van Gogh freak at that time, not me. I guess I caught it from him – like you got Beethoven off Ian Lewis. So here we came. It was the last really happy time we had together. But something wonderful happened to Aidan after that. Wonderful for him, not for me. He grew up at last in his own way. He met a woman and fell in love with her. Went through hell trying not to hurt me. But that was impossible. I had to be hurt. He had to live, to grow up in his way.'

'I'm sorry,' I said, thinking how strange were some of the things you found yourself saying sorry about. 'It happens, though. Not everybody knows themselves at... Well, whatever age he was.'

'I was twenty five,' Malcolm said. 'But Aidan was twenty-eight.' He gave me an odd look. The look may have been odd, but I understood its significance. 'I knew myself – from that point of view at least – when I was seven, despite a few untypical experiments in early adolescence. Stupidly I'd imagined that he knew himself equally well. But...' Malcolm gave one of the Gallic shrugs that he had had three years to practise.

I asked, 'And is he happy now? Do you know?'

'Most certainly he is. We exchange news at Christmas. It's all most civilised. He married the girl. She was – is – French. They live in Lyon and are halfway towards their two point four children or whatever the recommended ration is.'

'And you?'

'Like you, I discovered the flip side of love. You know, at least I suppose you do, that when two people fall in love they each plant a knife in the heart of the other. But it's only when the knife is wrenched out that the blood flows.'

There was silence for a moment. Then he said very gently, 'Tell me about Anne. I mean, if you want to.'

'I'm not sure if I know how to. I really don't know what was going on in her mind. You've talked about love. Well, for five years I believed Anne and I loved each other. I knew we did. But now I don't know. How could I lose a certainty like that: something so basic? I mentioned a girl called Janie, forever knitting a scarf. She got married not long before we did and we used to keep in touch. Anne and I used to laugh about Janie and her husband just a little. They seemed so contented, their marriage had an almost banal quality. We imagined they missed out on the highs and lows of love and life and the more their contentment deepened the more we – as I see it now – looked down on the quality of their relationship. It was as if their good fortune was something contemptible, something of which only idiots were worthy. Our own was always tinged with a degree of cynicism that seemed the healthy result of our being sophisticated, intelligent people. It never occurred to us to be jealous of them. Nor did we consider the possibility – which I have only just begun to think about in the last few weeks – that they were truly in love and we were not.'

'Where is Anne now?' Malcolm asked quietly.

'She has a good job in the museum in Norwich. And I've heard she's got a new man. I suppose I'm pleased for her.'

'She's getting over it like a youngster, perhaps,' Malcolm said. He smiled and shook his head. 'That's what you said last night. Don't know if you remember that. That Ian Lewis had 'got over it as youngsters do'. I nearly took you up on it but didn't. How does anyone know who gets over what? And what about your friend Happy: wasn't he a youngster? I'll put it down to a slip of the tongue, or the carelessness of cognac.' He paused a second, then said, 'You too should try being a youngster one day.'

I didn't say anything to that. Malcolm plucked a couple of stalks of grass. Then he said, 'How do you feel about the boy now?'

That startled me a bit. 'Ian? I don't feel anything about him *now*, if you understand me, because I don't know what he's like now. But about him *then*, my feelings have gone through a few changes. At first I felt sorry for him, then, with all the bitterness of the divorce, I began to hate him. Later I managed to shut him out of my mind. I could even listen to Beethoven without him coming into my thoughts. The file was closed.'

'You've told me he had feelings for you,' Malcolm said. 'Are you quite sure, in your heart of hearts, that you had nothing of the same feeling for him?'

'It takes two to tango,' I said, 'and in that particular case only one of us wanted to. Still, the hard feelings have gone. I wish him well, wherever he is.'

Then another thought struck me. I hesitated before asking this, but then I did ask. 'You say Aidan found his heterosexual side as he grew older. How can you be sure that the same thing won't happen with Henri?'

'Because of Henri himself. I know you've hardly met him, but does he strike you as someone who'll change with the wind or the seasons?'

'I have to say, on a first impression, no, he doesn't. All the same...'

'Aidan never gave the same first impression, if that's what you're wondering. He was like mercury, if you want. Henri's like gold.'

'That's very pretty.'

'It's very true.'

I said, 'Then why the hell...?' It was impossible now, after the turn the conversation had taken, not to bring this up. 'What the fuck were we playing at last night – not just you, me as well?'

Malcolm was silent a moment and looked down. He plucked at another plant stem. At once the scent of lemon thyme filled the air. 'Last night was a mistake.' he said. 'And if you want me to say sorry, then sorry. Now I've said it. But I don't really mean it was a mistake as

you would understand a mistake. With your conventional rules and two point four children and divorce until
death.' He spoke bitterly all of a sudden.

I found myself speaking bitterly too. 'You talk of my
conventionality as if conventionality was something
criminal. You may despise it and laugh at it if you want
to but you can never say that it's wrong.'

'No,' said Malcolm, 'I can't. Unless, unless, just
possibly it's the wrong convention. The wrong
convention for you.' His tone softened. 'No, David, I'm
sorry. There's nothing criminal, as you put it, about your
particular conventionality. The only person it can hurt
from now on is you.'

My hackles rose. 'What the hell's that supposed to
mean? That I've hurt people in the past? By responding
to them differently from the way you would have?
That's monstrously arrogant. That I've upset you by not
wanting to sleep with you? That I'm missing out on
something if I don't? Christ Almighty!'

'No, I don't mean that,' Malcolm said. 'It's just that
you seem trapped by this idea that everybody has to be
treated, or to behave, the same.'

'You think I do?'

'And how! You think I was out of order last night
because I have a relationship with someone else and that
means no sleeping around elsewhere. Wrong. That's
what I meant when I said I hadn't made a mistake as you
would understand it. In my book I made a mistake last

night because I have a relationship *with Henri* and *that particular relationship* means no sleeping with other people. Even (don't hit me) with a friend as delightful as you.'

I said more quietly, 'I admit that I behaved stupidly myself. It wasn't just you that was out of order. I was drunk and crazy and...' I stopped and stared down at the grass for a moment, as if I'd seen an abyss being opened up by my own words. Then, with a struggle, I pulled my thoughts together. 'I also admit it was stupid of me to give you a kiss, even in fun, two days ago. It was just high spirits, but it gave you the wrong message, and I apologise for that. But...' I groped desperately for something that would make sense. 'I got out of your bed principally for the one reason that you've dismissed as unworthy of your notice. And it's not particular to us. Where I'm concerned it's general. I do not sleep with men. Ever. I don't wish to and I'm not going to. Full stop.' But even as I heard myself say it I found myself wondering if I was really telling the truth.

Malcolm decided to change the subject. 'Sometimes,' he began slowly, 'it seems as if life, or God, or fate or whatever you like to call it, knocks down the building you've been trying to make of your life and gives you the chance to begin it again. When Aidan left me it was as if the linchpin had been pulled out of the structure I'd fondly called my life and that all I had left were the building blocks. However bad things get, however broken, you never lose those building blocks. Your past goes to build your future; none of it is wasted. I'm only beginning to understand that now.' He got up and retreated to the other side of the cypress tree from where I presently heard the sound of him pissing. It was as sure an indication as any that the discussion was closed.

THIRTEEN

Things could easily have gone downhill from then on: our conversation reduced to scratchy bickering, our companionship turned to mutual irritation, that holiday intimacy that Malcolm likened one day to a brightly coloured bubble hardened to an amber prison. Somehow none of this took place. Perhaps the climate was to thank, our northern souls finding it impossible to remain quarrelsome for long under this brief interrogation by the southern sun. In fact the heat lessened somewhat over the next few days though the weather did not break – for us tourists the only improvement to be wished. Travelling became supportable once more, while the dazzling envelope of colour and light in which we moved didn't fade at all. On the contrary the colour seemed to etch itself more and more deeply into the slate of my mind.

We explored the flatlands of the Camargue, circumnambulated the walled town of Aigues Mortes and drove eventually into Arles. Here were fewer tangible links with Van Gogh than at St-Rémy – two world wars had seen to that – but the unresolved tensions of primary colour that inspired his canvasses were everywhere still: green oleanders, yellow stucco and orange brick; blue and violet sky. Swept up one picturesque narrow street on a flood tide of clicking cameras, we were relieved at one point to be washed up in a shop doorway, but momentarily puzzled to see someone beckoning to us from the relative darkness of the shop's interior. It only took me a second, though, to remember the fine art dealer who had given us his card on the TGV.

Despite the crowds in the street his gallery was not busy. Day-trippers did not spend a lot on fine art, he told us. Perhaps time was hanging heavily on his hands: his pleasure at seeing us seemed disproportionate to our brief acquaintance. At any rate he was more than happy to show us the paintings on his walls, while a curly-headed blond youth did discreet sentry duty behind the fine mahogany table that it would have been *lèse-majesté* to describe as either a counter or a cash desk. Most of the canvasses depicted the flat, wind-ruffled landscapes of the Camargue, though here and there were street scenes recognizable as being Avignon, Aix and other towns we had passed through. Malcolm suddenly pointed to a painting of the Café de Paris, the 'route-map' bar, in L'Isle sur la Sorgue. Clearly someone else had remarked on its resemblance to Van Gogh's *Terrasse du Café le Soir* and had highlighted the resemblance by painting it from the same angle and at the same time of evening. Familiar yellow lights gleamed out of neighbouring dormers. 'We were there a few nights ago,' Malcolm explained to the gallery owner.

'C'est romantique, n'est-ce pas?' he replied. Then, after a pause while he gave us as thorough an appraisal with his dark and expert eyes as if he were judging the merits of a double portrait, he asked us if we would like to see the other part of his collection downstairs. The

young man at the table looked up when he heard this invitation made, but then returned to his previous occupation of observing through the window the passers-by in the sunny street outside.

Downstairs, in an even darker exhibition room we found ourselves in the centre of a collection of photographs whose subject matter – it did not come as a surprise to me now – was the male nude. The style owed a lot to Robert Maplethorpe. Malcolm was clearly delighted, while I found myself trying not to think too hard about my own reaction. Until I was pulled up short by one particular picture. It was simple in the extreme. A blond-haired youth stood in a patchwork of sunshine and shadow, his back against the stone wall of what might have been a barn, his cock lolling, half-fat, against one downy thigh. Surely, surely, wasn't that familiar-looking form and face that of Ian Lewis?

'Who took that photo?' I asked hoarsely, too surprised to mask my desperate need to know. Malcolm peered over my shoulder at the photo, curious as to what had precipitated my reaction.

'Jean-Charles did. The young man you saw upstairs. He has a talent, has he not?'

I said, 'Do you know, I mean, would he remember who…? No, sorry, it doesn't matter. Just something that came into my head. Forget it. It doesn't matter.'

But the gallery owner, pleased with himself for picking up on the first of my signals, failed to register the second. 'Jean-Charles,' he called upstairs. 'Here a minute. Answer a question.' And the young man came pattering down the stairs.

'What was the name of this one?' asked the gallery owner.

'Oh…' The young man tapped his head. 'Oh gosh. It was, let me think … er … An English guy. Ian.'

'Ian?' queried Malcolm, who, after a few seconds of puzzled peering had just got to where I had arrived at once; he had been at a disadvantage when it came to recognizing the figure and face.

'Look, this really doesn't matter,' I said.

'I'm sure it was Ian,' said the young man. 'In fact I think it may be written on the back.' With a certain amount of fuss he de-mounted the photograph from the wall and there, sure enough, was written on the back a date, a location and a name. The name was Ian. But the surname wasn't Lewis. The young man depicted was apparently called Ian Smart. 'There you are,' he said proudly. 'I thought I'd remembered right.'

There was a longish silence. Then the gallery owner broke it unexpectedly by saying, 'Look, why don't we all have lunch together?' And so we did. My pleasure in the expensive restaurant meal that followed was tempered by the knowledge that Jean-Charles and the gallery owner (whose name was on his visiting card inside my wallet, but there was no way I could take it out to remind myself what it was) both took me and

Malcolm to be a couple. Still, it was always agreeable to be treated to a meal by someone whose wallet was fatter than your own. We had rose-tinted trout with almonds, a *vin gris* (also pink) from the nearby hills, and a *coulis* of summer berries, and when we parted company afterwards it was in a friendly spirit.

That evening we returned to St-Rémy where we watched late-hunting swifts swirling like bats among the blossoming stars and, from the safety of a seat among the plane trees we tried, by screwing our eyes half shut, to cause the celestial bodies that watched over the town to dance as the artist had seen them do.

We knew we were going to have to talk about what had happened at the art dealer's shop at some point. In the end it was I who brought it up.

'You said, after we'd met him on the train, that that art dealer obviously fancied one of us. Well, I thought you were being a bit fanciful, if you like. Until he invited us downstairs, of course, and then it became pretty clear.'

'How clear?' asked Malcolm.

'Well that he obviously did fancy one of us. Though it wasn't clear to me which one.'

Malcolm said, 'Now I think about it, I'm not sure it was quite like that. It may have just been the idea of the two of us together that he found attractive. Nothing more alarming than that.'

'I see,' I said. I actually found it more alarming to hear Malcolm so breezily accept what I had reluctantly realised that lunchtime: that other people might take the two of us for a gay couple.

'But what surprised me,' Malcolm changed the subject, 'was what on earth made you think you were looking at a picture of Ian Lewis this morning. I mean, I know you'd seen him swimming once in the nude, but…'

'It doesn't matter,' I said. 'Just a mistake.'

We resumed our travels. We explored Aix and Carpentras and the slopes of Mont Ventoux. The private bubble in which we journeyed and lived remained un-punctured by any further adventures that might have troubled my comfortable view of my sexual orientation. Bedtimes returned once more to being – if not sober, then at least chaste. Then, on the last night of our tour, when we'd returned the car to its ring-road garage and were back at the Hotel Bristol, I woke during the night to find Malcolm's silhouette at one of the windows, leaning half out and smoking a cigarette. His naked form was all in shadow except for where the street-lighting picked out the line of his shoulders and forearm in pale ivory – a far cry from the bricky hue that the sun now painted him by day.

'Anything wrong, Malcolm? Can't you sleep?' I said.

'Uh-huh.'

'Why not?'

The silhouette turned to face me. 'Thinking about you, actually.'

'I see,' I said.

The silhouette took a pull on its cigarette. A pinprick of red light intensified in the dark. 'You're gay, David. A poof. A fairy. A faggot. Queer. Call it what the hell you like; it makes no difference. That is you. I know that and so, now, do you.'

'What?!' I thought Malcolm had gone mad. I sat bolt upright.

'I thought the other day that I would never dare to tell you so straight out. I thought the risk to our friendship would outweigh any possible gain to you. Just now I changed my mind. So I've told you what I'm thinking.'

'Malcolm, that's some accusation!'

'Not an accusation. An observation. A diagnosis, if you like. Even if incorrect it wouldn't become an accusation. It's not something bad to be. And don't act shocked; I'm hardly the first person to tell you. Even your wife...'

'Not something bad to be? For you, no, because that's the way you're made. But it would be for me; I'm not like you, don't you see? It's you now who tries to generalise all the time, not me. And don't go quoting my wife to me. My real friends have always believed me rather than her. I thought that you...'

'Come on, come on. That's baby-talk. It's crap.'

'Malcolm, what is this?'

'Have a cigarette. Catch.' Malcolm threw me one. 'And you'd better light it yourself in the circumstances.' He took a fresh one himself. 'OK. Let's get one thing out of the way first. I've always liked the way you look, the way you talk, the way you are. Fancied you, in brief. But, except for that bit of stupidity on my part the other night, that's water under the bridge and we can leave it out of the argument.

'But since then I've been doing some thinking about those two ghosts in your life that you can't shake off. Two men. Happy, who killed himself after seeing a blackmailed homosexual put in prison just a couple of weeks after falling in love with you...'

'That's a wild guess, Malcolm. Pure imagination, conjecture.'

'And there's Ian, the kid with teeth. You think you're really screwed up by Anne and the divorce. Bullshit. Divorce takes a lot longer to happen than a love bite yet you told me about your divorce in two sentences and took ten minutes over that little episode with that kid. And remember I've only heard the case for the defence. David, it's Ian and Happy that you're screwed up about. Not Anne but those two. Those two and yourself.'

'Go to bed,' I said. 'I'm not listening. Go to sleep.'

Malcolm did not obey. He left the window and crossed to his bed, then sat down on the far end of it.

'It was lovely that you agreed to come to Provence with me, to share a bedroom with a gay bloke. I've loved watching you fall in love with the colour and the light. I loved it that you jumped across the stream at L'Isle sur la Sorgue and gave me a kiss. I know that you felt the electric charge as keenly as I did when that Italian came down all naked from that Van Gogh window. So keenly that just for a few minutes you were almost as ready to have sex with me as I was with you...'

I tried to bluster my way out. I said, 'Your imagination beats a spotty adolescent's. Talk about wishful thinking! And your memory's about as objective as ... as...'

'David, David,' Malcolm said quietly, 'just be yourself at last, that's all. Now I'm sorry. You may possibly never forgive me for saying all that. You may never understand why I did. Look, I need some air. I'm going out for a walk.' He began to dress himself.

I was lost for words. My cigarette finished, I lay flat once more, pulling the sheets around me like a child, though the night was still hot. I found my tongue again just as Malcolm reached the door. 'Don't try to change people,' I said. 'To warp them into your own image. That is wrong. Very.'

Malcolm stopped, his hand already on the handle. 'It is wrong,' he said with great feeling. 'My God, it is. I couldn't agree more. But I've said nothing to try to change you; I've only tried to point to who you are. And if by any chance the cap doesn't fit, well, you won't be wearing it anyway. It was only an inspired guess. If there's anything that needs changing it's way out of my reach; I couldn't do anything there even if I wanted to. I leave that to you. To you and your ghosts. Now I'm going out. I've got the key and I won't be long.' He paused for a second. Then he said, 'The real David, I begin to think, is even now not really angry or surprised by what I've said.' Then he opened the door and went out. I didn't hear him return.

In the morning we realised that we'd forgotten to set the mosquito-screens at the windows. We took the souvenirs of this oversight back with us to Paris.

FOURTEEN

Kilometre by kilometre the progress of twelve days ago was reversed. From south to north, from a great light to a lesser, from mountain horizons to the plain.

After our exchange of words the previous night the atmosphere between us might have been frosty. It wasn't. It was quite sober: that's to be expected on the return from a holiday, especially when you're returning to the northern, from the southern part of France. But there was no animosity between us. We had had to agree to differ. Malcolm mistakenly believed that I was gay – a closet case or worse. I knew, of course, that I was not.

We returned to Malcolm's wonderful flat, next door to where Vincent had lived with his brother, in the rue Lepic. Henri had returned from Vichy a couple of hours earlier. I was touched by the rapture with which Malcolm and Henri greeted each other. And I wasn't surprised when they excused themselves for a private half-hour in their bedroom. They seemed almost to be asking my permission to do this, Malcolm asking diffidently, 'Would you mind very much if...?'

Laughingly I told him not to worry. I said I would take myself out for a walk. They gave me a key to let myself in with when I came back.

I took myself up the steep rue Lepic, to where it entered the heart of Montmartre at the Place du Tertre. Painters sat at easels, capturing on canvas the famous and picturesque buildings around them that had been made famous by generations of painters before them, going all the way back to the Impressionists. I sat and had an espresso at a pavement table, watching scissor artists cutting out profiles of tourists from black paper at lightning speed. It seemed a long way from Van Gogh.

Around another corner I found myself on the tourist-filled terrace in front of the white-domed Basilica of Sacré Coeur, standing at the rails and overlooking the whole of central Paris. There were the towers and arrow-spire of Notre Dame, the golden dome of the Invalides, the Pantheon, the Opera… and those wonderful double-sloped grey rooftops and their dozens of chimney-pots. I thought of that lovely film, The Red Balloon, and how it ended with the little boy flying, lifted by hundreds of balloons across the rooftops of Paris… Across the very vista I was looking at. I looked at my watch. I'd been out for forty-five minutes. By the time I got back Malcolm and Henri would have had time to make love at least twice. I turned away from the view and made my way back down the hill in the slanting evening sun.

Later we went out for a meal at a favourite restaurant of theirs in the rue de Clignancourt. 'I've looked at those Van Gogh reproductions on your walls again,' I said. (I'd had a few spare minutes by myself in the salon after I came back from my walk.) 'I see them with new eyes, with new feelings almost, now I've been to Provence. Actually walked through the streets he painted. Seen inside the asylum at St-Rémy. Looked at the stars through the cypress trees at night…'

Nineteen-year-old Henri said unexpectedly, 'Maybe it won't just be Van Gogh you'll look at with new eyes now you've been down there.' He didn't elaborate and I didn't ask him to. I knew exactly what he meant. Inevitably Malcolm had talked to him about me while I'd been out, walking up to Montmartre and back. They wouldn't have only been having sex.

'Maybe,' I said.

I had one more day to spend in Paris before returning to England. Malcolm had some teaching to do, and Henri would be back behind his computer screen in the travel agent's where he worked. Over breakfast they both made suggestions about parts of the city I might like to visit. I said vaguely that I might wander around by the Seine. The Ile de la Cité, the Louvre, the Place de la Concorde, perhaps… Henri told me, with a straight face, that I ought to include a stroll along the riverbank quai des Tuileries.

I took the bus that dived down a picturesque route past unexpectedly quaint churches and houses hundreds of years old and then, after a walk in which I got pleasantly lost a few times, I found myself at the river. Everywhere the views were like paintings into which you could simply walk. It's difficult to explain, but there is something particularly magical about the heart of Paris.

I walked around the Ile de la Cité, enjoying its

changing perspectives; the spires of the Conciegerie, Notre Dame and the Sainte Chapelle appearing to do a stately dance around the sky together as I moved from place to place; the river appearing in teasing glimpses between green willow trees; the quays beyond... I remembered Henri's recommendation of the quai des Tuileries. I took a quick look at the map Malcolm had lent me and made my way there through the late July heat.

The quai des Tulieries turned out to be a lengthy pathway along the river, beneath the wall of the Tuileries gardens. It also turned out to be – Henri had deliberately not told me this, evidently – a major gay cruising ground.

Had I wanted to charge people for telling them the time I could have filled my pockets with francs. I could also have given away the contents of several packets of cigarettes... Men were everywhere, dressed in swimming-trunks of the scantiest proportions, the remainder of their clothes presumably stuffed into the backpacks they all either carried, if they were walking about, or used as pillows or back-rests if they were lying down taking the sun.

Some had formed themselves into pairs and were standing half-hidden among the trees, embracing, their tongues down each other's throats, their hands down inside each other's swimming-trunks. Other pairs were lying on top of each other on the ground, trunks pulled down a little way, bottoms exposed to the sun... I found myself reacting quite strongly to this scene, to this new canvas I'd unexpectedly walked into: this new window I found myself walking through. I felt queasy. I didn't like it. And yet I did. I was guiltily excited by what was going on around me. I felt my penis thicken in my pants. I found myself wondering what the place would be like at night…

Had Malcolm ever walked down here at night? I wondered. Between his break-up with Aidan and meeting Henri? And what of Henri himself? Henri who was only nineteen… Having posed the questions I discovered that I didn't want to know the answers. Yet other questions crowded in. Was this the place Happy's nocturnal rambles would have brought him to, given life and time? Aged nineteen, wandering Durham's riverbanks at night, had he, unsuspected by innocent me, actually already been doing this? A few days ago, I would have said no, of course not. But now, after everything that had happened in Provence, the whole of the past seemed up for renegotiation. It rose up before me and bristled like a porcupine, every quill a question. What if? With a mixture of relief and a curious disappointment I reached the steps that led up to the bridge

I went on mulling this over as I walked northwards through the heterosexual streets. Supposing all of that was true about Happy, including what Malcolm had said nearly two weeks ago about his having been in love with me. What did that say about me? Had I been in love with Happy too? Malcolm had also suggested that. How could I, aged twenty-eight, have had no inkling of that before coming to France?

Malcolm had suggested I was gay. Gay without knowing it! Impossible, surely. And yet Malcolm's Aidan hadn't known about *his* own disposition till he was twenty-eight. Still, there was an enormous difference between our cases. Aidan's discovery had not occurred in a vacuum, there had been nothing abstract or intellectual about it. He had met someone, a woman, another human being, who had been... Been what? A mirror in which he had seen himself for the first time without distortion perhaps; a window through which his future had come into focus for the first time; a sudden glimpse of the sun without dark glasses? But a human being, a person. That above all.

Then I found myself thinking about Ian. Had he grown up gay in the end? What was his life like now? Did he spend his spare time doing what I'd so recently witnessed in the sunshine under the walls of the gardens of the Tuileries? It was yet another disturbing line of thought.

Two nights ago I had defended myself easily against Malcolm's over-the-top harangue, if not in words at least in my own mind. My fortress walls had stood. Malcolm physically present, a naked friend with a sun-peeled nose being histrionic in a hotel room, had left me relatively unruffled. But Malcolm's words seemed more powerful now, now that I'd walked the quai des Tuileries, and had got an erection as I'd walked and looked.

The French are quite something when it comes to food. At the end of his day's work Henri came home and prepared a meal for the three of us. He did eggs in aspic jelly for a starter. They came from a shop, admittedly, but he still had to wrap a warm cloth around their little moulds and get his timing right so as to get them out in one piece each. Within the jelly a slice of ham was wrapped around a soft-boiled egg, which spilt its gold contents prettily, like a liquid jewel, when you cut into it. Then pork tenderloin, *filet mignon* as he called it, served on a bed of tomatoes and courgettes. A selection of cheeses, then soft fruit with ice cream. I'd have taken my hat off, had I been wearing one.

'I did explore the quai des Tuileries,' I said as we were tucking into the first course.

'What did you think of it?' Henri asked with a bit of a twinkle in his eye.

'An eye-opener, to be honest,' I said. 'But interesting.' Then I added, because I knew that Malcolm would have told Henri some of this, 'Malcolm is determined to make a gay man out of me. I'm not sure he's going to meet with much success. I think it's the effect that Provence has on him. All that sun and light. Another twenty-four hours and he'd probably have been saying that even Van Gogh was gay!'

'Who knows?' said Henri, with a wicked half smile. 'And who knows what will be the effect on you of all that sun and light?'

Then he stretched his hand across the table towards my bare forearm, stopping his fingers a millimetre short of my skin but then running them up to my elbow through the hairs, rubbing those up the wrong way and triggering a miniature storm of static. The effect was electric, literally so, and magical. It stirred something among my deepest feelings: something I hadn't known about. And despite the presence of Malcolm at the table with us it was a wonderfully intimate contact. It prevented me from saying anything further on the subject we'd been talking about. And I had to admit, it felt very, very nice.

When I went to bed that night, a little fuzzy with wine and cognac, and closed my eyes, my mind was filled with a kaleidoscope of images. Most were of the nearly naked male bodies I'd seen enjoying themselves and each other in the sunshine on the quai des Tuileries. But among them came repeatedly the memory, very vividly, of the naked photo of the boy called Ian Smart, who looked like Ian Lewis: the photo that we'd seen in Arles, in the art dealer's shop.

I couldn't believe how brightly those pictures all filled my imagination then. There was so much colour, so much light. My sheets were the same ones I'd had when I spent my first night here a fortnight ago. They were still emblazoned with my map of France. Nobody would notice if I overlaid that with another one. With those pictures still filling my mind's eye powerfully I reached for my erect cock and started to masturbate.

FIFTEEN

Malcolm did manage to persuade me of one thing, at least. That I should do a training course in teaching English as a foreign language, just as he had done when he dropped out of school teaching a few years earlier. Then I could work anywhere in the world I wanted. I might not become rich but... He promised me that if I wanted him to he would introduce me to the powers that be at the business school where he taught in Paris.

I made enquiries once I was back in England and a few days later, after an interview at a centre in London, I was enrolled on a short course. That didn't begin for another month. We were now in August. That August in England was good, weather-wise, and I would have been quite happy whiling the spare month away in my home country, seeing friends and doing not very much. But I'd been spoiled by Van Gogh's land of light and colour. I hankered after Provence. After a few days I went back.

I went the slow way this time, as, having recently returned from a two-week holiday with hotels to pay for, I was counting my pennies. I went by train as far as Dover, then crossed to Calais by hovercraft. From there I travelled by long-distance coach. One took me into central Paris, another took me out the other side and – in the course of a long and not very comfortable night – all the way to Arles.

Why Arles rather than Avignon or Aix, or St Rémy

come to that? The answer was something I was reluctant to admit to myself. I wanted to see Jean-Charles, the young assistant in the art dealer's shop, and get to the bottom of the mystery that was Ian Smart – or maybe Ian Lewis. I didn't tell Malcolm I was returning to France. And I certainly wasn't going tell him about that.

I awoke in my bouncing coach seat that next morning to see that we were sailing across a sea of sunflowers that were looking towards the dawn. Happy had talked of celestial Tippex when describing the effects of snow. I don't know. Does Tippex also come in gold?

The coach drew into the bus station at Arles. I blundered off it and went in search of coffee and croissants. The morning was cold, although it was August. A chill wind was blowing in off the Camargue. It was still only seven o'clock. I spun my coffee and croissants out as long as I could. Then I walked around the town. What time did art galleries open? I wondered. I guessed, not till ten o'clock.

Little by little the wind dropped, and then reversed itself. The scent of thyme and lavender blew into the town's streets from the blue hills inland, and the day warmed up. I dropped in at a couple more cafés while I loitered. I felt I was getting to know the town a bit. Had I been a painter I could have painted it.

I found the street where the art gallery was. I braced myself and opened the door. There sat curly blond Jean-

Charles at his sentry-box desk. Although we'd had lunch together a mere two weeks ago I didn't presume on his remembering me without Malcolm, out of context. *'Bonjour, Jean-Charles,'* I said.

'Bonjour,' he said, and hesitated no more than a second before smiling, and adding, 'David.' It was a good start.

'How are you?' I asked him in French.

'I am good,' he said in English. 'You went back to England, did you not?'

'Yes,' I said. 'But now I have come back to France.'

'That is very soon,' he said. 'But we are honoured by that.'

'I came back,' I said, 'and please don't misunderstand me, but I came back especially to see you. There is some information I want from you. I need to pick your brains.'

Jean-Charles's rather beautiful young face puckered into a frown. 'Pick my brains? What is that?'

'Sorry,' I said. 'It's an expression. It just means there are some questions I want to ask you, and I need your advice.'

He nodded his understanding and his frown was replaced by a new smile as quickly as if I'd flicked a switch.

'Tirez, monsieur.' Fire away, he said. 'Although I

think I can imagine. It's about that photograph.'

'Précisément,' I said.

'I remember the moment very clearly,' Jean-Charles said. 'I had the impression you thought you knew the guy. When I told you his first name you were – how to say? – bouleversé, but in a good way. But when I told you the second name you were deceived, *n'est-ce pas?'*

'Yes,' I said. Disappointed was what he'd meant.

'After that day we met,' Jean-Charles said, 'I thought about the thing a lot. I went back in my mind to remember how I met the guy and how it happened that I took the photograph. Would you like me to tell you what I remember?'

'Yes please,' I said.

'It was last summer,' he began. 'I was walking along the river out in the country near here, with my camera, taking photos of the nature. I saw three young guys, maybe nineteen years, who had taken off their clothes and were playing by the edge of the water and in the water, running in and out and laughing. They saw me. I was wearing … well, just shorts and boots and my camera round my shoulder…'

I found I could imagine the scene only too easily. Jean-Charles would have been halfway between their age and mine, I thought. He was probably about twenty-four…

'They asked me in English if I would like to take a photo of them. I thought they were serious and I started to ask them to move into a group. But then they changed their *avis*, and said, no, please do not.

'But one of them – he was actually the handsomest – came up to me and said I could take his photo naked, if I wanted, and if I would give him two hundred francs. I said that was a lot of money, and I offered him one hundred. He accepted that and I took the photo you saw. Of him with the tree behind him. I would have liked to take him to a studio and make many more pictures of him. Of him and his … his *bite*, how do you say?'

'His cock,' I said. 'Or his dick, if you like.'

Jean-Charles smiled. 'His cock or his dick if I like. I will remember that. OK. After that we talked a little. He told me his name was Ian Smart – though I remember he hesitated before saying 'Smart'. It was like he invented that very quick. He told me they were three friends who studied at university in London and were here on holiday. I asked Ian if he wanted a copy of the photo. He thought for a little bit, then he said yes, and he gave me his address. It was not easy to find a pen and some paper, with nobody very well dressed, but one boy found those things in his backpack. Then we parted. I never saw them again.'

'And did you send him a copy of the photo?' I asked.

'Yes,' said Jean-Charles. 'He never wrote to say thank you, so I do not know if he received it.'

'And did you … have you still got… his address?'

Jean-Charles made a little grimace. 'I had the fear you would ask me that question,' he said. 'And that you would not like my answer. No. I am very sorry. I do not have his address now.'

We both realised that my research had hit the buffers. There was nowhere else to go with this. There was a silence between us. I realised at that moment that Jean-Charles had been talking to me in the way he would talk to another gay man. He had made the assumption that I was gay, and treated me accordingly. He continued to do so now.

'Tonight we have a *vernissage*,' he said. 'Would you like to come to it?'

'What is a *vernissage*?' I asked.

'It is when we open a new exhibition and we invite people, the people who buy art from us, also their friends, and especially people who are a bit rich, and there is wine and canapés…'

'I understand,' I said. 'It's called a private view in English.'

'You can come if you would like,' he said again. 'You do not have to buy a picture. And there will be good wine. Your friend … Malcolm, is it? … can come too. He is here with you in Arles?'

Sometimes it was nice to be mistaken for a gay man.

'He isn't here,' I said. 'He is in Paris with his French boyfriend, Henri. Malcolm was never my boyfriend. We are just old friends who studied together. I'm here on my own this time. So, thank you for the invitation. I'll certainly come. I'd really like that.' I was really touched. 'I need to find somewhere to stay in the town, though.'

Jean-Charles gave me an appraising look. 'How long will you stay in Arles?'

'I think just one night. Maybe two.' I smiled. 'I have to go home after that. I can't spend another week in hotels, after my last visit. I'm not even a little bit rich.'

'There is a sofa at my place,' he said, a bit diffidently. 'You could sleep on that for a few nights, if you wanted. It's my parents' house actually, but they are away. At least it would be free.'

'It's a very kind offer,' I said. 'May I accept?'

I spent most of that day with Jean-Charles and with his boss, whose name – I had to ask Jean-Charles to remind me of this – was Marc. They showed me the Place du Forum, in which the café that Van Gogh had made famous still stood. Even so, it looked less like his golden picture of it than the Café de France in L'Isle-sur-la-Sorgue, where Malcolm and I had got so drunk a few weeks back. Perhaps that was a question of the time of day, the state of the light … or how much we'd had to drink.

They showed me the rebuilt Yellow House, where Vincent had lived. Where he'd covered the walls with his sunflower paintings in readiness for Gaugin's visit. Marc bought lunch for Jean-Charles and me. In the afternoon I repaid their hospitality, present, future and past, by helping to hang the pictures for the exhibition that would open that evening.

Most of the paintings I was hanging depicted summer landscapes of Provence and the Loire: landscapes that were bright with lads and lasses, and golden with ripening corn. It was a very life-affirming collection, I thought. The pictures did my heart good. And hanging them did my muscles good.

A young man passed the open doorway at one moment. He stopped and looked in. He was wearing ancient orange bell-bottoms and a football shirt and he carried his possessions in a small plastic sack. He looked no more than twenty and his face had a composure and a serenity that reminded me, when I caught sight of it, of a picture I had seen in a book about the Louvre: Watteau's 'Gilles', the portrait of a simple clown. Jean-Charles saw me looking at the young man, who moved off down the street at that moment. 'He's a homeless guy,' Jean-Charles explained. 'He sleeps in doorways around here. He appeared just a few weeks ago. We've tried to speak to him, but he's mute and deaf. The other thing about him is, he's interested in art. He looks always through the windows here. And he can draw and paint a bit. Sometimes he sells a sketch to tourists in the Place de la République.'

'He sounds interesting,' I said.

I met a lot of interesting people at the *vernissage.* The evening pushed my French to its absolute limit, but that also did me good. Among the people I got talking to was … Marc's wife.

You don't expect gay men to have wives, yet Marc, who I had no doubt was a gay man, did have a wife. Her name was Brigitte. There was no end, I thought, to the complexity of sexuality and life. Malcolm had been right about some things, I now realised, and I'd been wrong about them. I would see him soon, I hoped, and humbly tell him that. Now Marc's wife and I were talking about Paris…

She broke off suddenly from a story she was telling me about a recent visit to the Opera there, her attention distracted by a figure in the doorway. 'I wonder who is that?' she asked.

I looked. 'It's a young deaf mute,' I said, 'and he's interested in art.' I felt absurdly pleased with myself for being able to tell her something about someone in her town that I knew but she did not. I went on and told her everything Jean-Charles had told me about him.

Brigitte nodded approvingly. 'Perhaps he'd like a glass of champagne,' she said, surprising me a bit. 'I'll ask him in anyway.' She went out to do just that and immediately, as if filling a vacuum, a young friend of Jean-Charles whom I'd been introduced to earlier appeared at my other elbow and topped up my glass.

Brigitte returned a moment later with the young man in orange bell-bottoms following obediently like a dog. 'He doesn't speak,' she said. 'But he understands. He isn't deaf. His name's Raoul.'

'How do you know that if he doesn't speak?' asked Jean-Charles's friend.

'It's engraved on a chain round his neck,' said Brigitte.

'Is the address there too?' the friend asked. 'We could send him home by post.'

'Don't be naughty,' said Brigitte. 'Find him a chair and I'll look for a glass for him.'

A few moments later the young man was equipped with a chair, a glass of champagne and a plate of canapés, and being fussed over by all the arty well-dressed guests.

'Just look at that tableau,' said Marc, joining me. He gestured to where Raoul sat, expressionless and looking more than ever like Watteau's painting. On his left Brigitte was talking to him painstakingly, framing questions so that they could be answered with either a nod or a shake of the head. On his right crouched Jean-Charles's friend, looking up at him intently like a disciple at the feet of a guru or else a painter sizing up the face as a possible model for some religious subject. 'I suppose the symbolism doesn't need pointing out,'

Marc said.

I thought about this. 'Perhaps it does, for me,' I said.

'Oh, I don't know,' said Marc. 'Blessed are the poor, perhaps, or blessed are the meek. Blessed are those who hunger and thirst – and blessed are the pure in heart. Theirs is the Kingdom anyway. We don't need to be very religious to realise that.'

Later in the evening Jean-Charles came up, with Raoul in tow, and caught me by the arm. 'Come with me,' he said. 'We're going to show this *mec* the photos downstairs.'

I said, 'Are you quite sure they'll be up his street? His cup of tea?'

Jean-Charles nodded gravely. 'I think so. Sometimes you just get a feeling about things. You know?'

The three of us walked down the stairs together. Jean-Charles had been right. The photos were very much up Raoul's street. I saw him smile for the first time as he looked in turn at each of us, pointing out interesting things in each of the photographs. Sometimes it was an interesting bit of background that caught his eye, or else he approved of the overall composition: the unity of the piece. But as often as not the thing that grabbed his attention in each photograph, and that he would point to, grinning cheekily at both of us, was the size or elegance of some young man's naked cock. Or *bite* as Jean-Charles had taught me to say in French.

We came to the picture of Ian Smart, or Ian Lewis, and he pointed approvingly at that particular young man's cock. I spoke then. I couldn't help myself. 'I think I knew that young man. He was a friend of mine once. And yes, he has a beautiful *bite*.'

SIXTEEN

It was late when we finished clearing up, and Jean-Charles and I walked back to his parents' house.

I had made an assumption, I discovered, without realising it. I'd assumed that because Jean-Charles had a friend whom I'd met and talked to, that friend must be not only gay but also Jean-Charles's boyfriend, his *copain*. I assumed that the three of us would go back to the parents' house, where I'd be given the sofa to sleep on as I'd been promised, while the other two, taking advantage of the parents' absence, would head off to Jean-Charles's room together, discreetly shutting the door behind them as they went.

I was wrong about some of that. Jean-Charles's friend was met by his girlfriend, his *copine*, who arrived at the door just as the party was breaking up. They drove off together in a Citroen Deux Chevaux. Raoul had taken his leave some time before that. On returning from the delights of the basement gallery he had reverted to being his previous quiet self, his face serene and unsmiling once again, though beautiful still, I had to admit. He had bowed slightly, in an almost Japanese kind of way, to both Jean-Charles and me as he turned for the door and made his way out into the dark. An hour or more passed after that before Jean-Charles and I left.

The walk was not a long one, Jean-Charles assured me. In the course of it we were brought up short. We spotted what looked like a bundle of clothes on the pavement. It was the bright orangeness of some of them that caused us to take a closer look. We were not looking at a bundle of clothes, we discovered, but at the silent, serious young man who wore the name Raoul on a chain round his neck. His shoes, together with his plastic bag of possessions, were stowed under the back of his head, where they formed an approximately theft-proof pillow. Jean-Charles felt in his pocket and found two ten-franc coins. Very gently he placed the money in one of Raoul's shoes, making every effort not to wake the sleeper and taking care that they were hidden from passing eyes by Raoul's thick hair. I felt myself shamed into doing the same thing. I knelt down too, and parted with twenty francs of my own. The price of three small beers or two sandwiches. We stood up and continued our walk.

A little later Jean-Charles said to me, 'Sorry, but I need urgently to piss.'

I said, 'You go ahead.'

He turned into the angle of a wall and got out his cock, which he made no attempt to hide from me. If anything the opposite was the case. But, just in case he was embarrassed about this, I followed his example, turning towards the bit of wall next to him, and unzipped my own jeans. Then for a minute we urinated side by side in a companionable silence that was broken only by the surprisingly loud sizzling of our two streams as they hit the wall and pavement.

We finished and zipped back up.

'We are nearly there,' said Jean-Charles as we resumed our walk. 'It was just that I could not wait.'

'Moi non plus,' me neither, I said. That wasn't true on my part: I could have waited easily. I wondered whether it was true on his.

A second later he put his arm lightly around my shoulder and I put mine around his.

I'd just seen this young man's dick. He'd as good as shown it off. I had to admit I was excited by the sight. It looked very nice.

I'd been excited by a lot of things this evening, though. The conviviality of the atmosphere. The champagne. The reaction of Raoul – which I hadn't expected – to the photos of young nude men in the basement. His reaction to the naked body of Ian Lewis … if it was Ian Lewis… My own reaction to it.

We arrived at the door of a substantial nineteenth century house and unhooked our arms from each other as Jean-Charles got his key out. Inside, the house was large and grandly furnished. Jean-Charles took me on a very quick tour of it. He was obviously proud to be showing it off. He showed me the inside of his bedroom. I noticed that he gave me time to clock the fact that he had a double bed.

'Une pour la route?' he asked me. Did I want a small night-cap? 'I had better not open champagne,' he said,

sounding apologetic. 'My parents…'

I said I'd accept whatever was going, and he poured us a small glass each of red wine from a bottle that had been opened the previous night.

We sat in the salon to drink it. Beneath a moulded ceiling and a dripping chandelier. Amidst a certain amount of gilt and plush. We sat next to each other on the sofa. We raised and clinked our glasses and said *Santé*. 'You are very kind, Jean-Charles,' I said.

He said, 'And you, David, are very nice.'

He reached forward a little and placed the palm of his hand on my thigh, at the same time looking very firmly into my eyes to see if I was OK with that.

It turned out that I was. I wouldn't have expected to be, but I was OK with that. I'd guessed that Jean-Charles was a few years younger than me. Whatever your sexuality, it's always flattering when a younger person behaves like that. 'How old are you?' I asked him.

'Twenty-four,' he said. 'And you?'

I said, 'I'm twenty-eight.'

Jean-Charles had given me about half a minute to remove my thigh from under his hand politely if I wanted to. He'd had time to conclude that I didn't want to do that. He started to stroke my thigh back and forth. I wriggled a few inches closer to him on the sofa and placed my own hand on his thigh, quite near the crotch.

His body stiffened for a second and he looked at me, trying to read my thoughts from my face. Then he relaxed and ran his hand across to where my cock and balls were. He felt them carefully through the denim, working out with his fingers exactly where everything was. He said, 'You have a very nice … cock.'

I said, 'It was small when you saw it out in the street.'

He said, 'It was still very nice.'

I recognised a cue when I heard one. I said, 'Yours was small too, but I still thought it was nice.' We leaned in towards each other and began to kiss.

There is something very special about that glass of wine that you know will be the last one you drink before you start doing something else. We didn't want to rush things – and yet we did. We compromised. Standing, we took each other's clothes off with one hand apiece, clutching our glasses of wine in the other hand and occasionally drinking from them as we progressed. Occasionally we had to cheat, and put the glasses down while we attended to some detail of clothing that was not amenable to being unfastened by a single hand. Belt-buckle. Shoe-laces. Then we finished the last drops of our wine and went naked up the stairs to bed with wagging dicks.

We got into bed and began to play with each other. We touched heads and necks, and backs and arms and thighs and buttocks. We reached down to feel each other's tough taut calves. For a second at a time we stroked each other's cock.

This was as far as I'd gone with Malcolm that drunken night. I wasn't drunk tonight, though I was relaxed and cheered by drink. I wondered what would happen next. What would we negotiate? I was the older one. Was it up to me to decide, despite my lack of experience of sex with other guys, exactly what we did? I decided to come clean. I said, *'Pour moi, c'est la premiere fois.'* Told him it was my first time with another man, and let him make what he would of that.

'But Ian…?' he said. 'Did you not…?'

'No,' I said. 'That's a long story. I'll tell you in the morning. Not tonight.'

He saw the sense of that. He said, 'We don't have to … as you say … fuck. We can just… You know.'

'Yes, I do know,' I said. 'For a first time I'll be happy with that.' And *that* was what we did.

It was lovely, I have to admit. In a way there was nothing new about it. It was more or less the same as I did with myself. People were beginning to use the word synergy about that time as a buzzword in business. Synergy meant two plus two made five, the definition went. Well, Jean-Charles and I experienced a kind of synergy that night. In our case it felt like one plus one made about six.

We came over each other's tummies, then held each

other wetly for a minute before Jean-Charles got out of bed and fetched a towel so that we could mop up. Then we held each other, asking no questions of ourselves or of each other, leaving the morning and its thorny thickets of doubts and problems to wait for us. In each other's arms we went to sleep.

'How long can you stay with me?' Jean-Charles asked me as we got dressed.

'I don't know,' I said. The question of expensive nights in hotels had been thrown out of the equation, but other things were left. 'When are your parents coming back?'

'Sunday night,' he said. 'They're in Italy right now. A sort of business plus holiday trip.'

Today was Wednesday. I weighed a few things up. 'I could stay till Sunday,' I said. 'I mean, if you wanted me to.' I smiled at him cautiously. 'And if we still like each other by Sunday.'

'I think we will,' he said.

Oh dear, I thought. And then we'll have a painful parting. He's young. He may not know that yet. I said, as gently as I could, 'I also hope we'll still like each other on Sunday. But we mustn't get too attached.'

'You are very cold, you English,' Jean-Charles said, though he said it with a friendly laugh. 'Very unromantic.'

'I'm just trying to be realistic,' I said. 'I'm older than you are. I know how easy it is to get hurt.'

'I understand,' he said. 'I know you want for the best.'

I walked round the corner of the bed to where he was standing half-dressed on his side of it. I gave him a little kiss and his still unclad cock a little tweak. 'What do you have for breakfast?' I asked.

I spent much of the day with Jean-Charles. In between walks around town on my own I stayed with him at the shop. A lot of his job was simply watching discreetly: checking that people didn't remove pictures from the walls, or leave smeary thumbprints on glass.

We talked a lot. I told him the whole story of Ian Lewis and me. That included the story of my marriage and divorce. He told me he'd had a boyfriend who he'd lived with. They'd split up and he'd gone back to his parents. 'Do your parents know you were in a gay relationship?' I asked him.

He looked a bit awkward. 'I don't think so,' he said. 'I think they just thought we shared a flat.'

'I see,' I said. 'That might be a bit difficult when you get another boyfriend and move out again,' I found myself thinking how difficult it must be for gay men who don't move away from their parental home towns.

Realising at that moment that that was why so many of them did.

'When I get another boyfriend…' he said. 'Or if…'

I was relieved he hadn't said that he'd now acquired one and that I was it. I said, 'You'll find someone very soon. I'm sure of it.'

It felt extraordinary to be talking like this. Talking about boyfriends to a man I'd slept with. A man I'd slept with. The weirdness, the improbability as I'd always thought, of that. And yet it had been nice. There was no doubt about that. I'd arranged quite calmly to sleep with him for the next four nights also. I thought again about gay men and their parents. At least I wouldn't have to confront mine with the information that I'd had a week-long fling with a gay young man. They lived six hundred miles away from Arles and even when I was in England we didn't see each other all that often. They'd certainly never need to know about this.

And when it came to flings with young men, well, anyway, I wouldn't be making a habit of it.

We lunched together, and in the evening we cooked together at his parents' house. It was funny observing Jean-Charles observing me in the kitchen. For the first time in his life, probably, he was watching an Englishman cook. He watched with a certain amount of disbelief as I filled a pan with water, put it on to boil, added salt, and weighed out pasta to cook in it. It was as though he hadn't previously imagined any English or other British person could do this without ruining the eventual dish. My *spaghetti al limone* was a revelation to him. The pasta was simply tossed in a mixture of lemon juice, virgin olive oil and lemon zest, with Parmesan grated on top. Jean-Charles was astonished when I actually pulled it off. 'It is impossible,' he said. 'I really am enjoying this.'

He was responsible for the next course. It was a veal cutlet with a green salad. I told him it was the sort of thing I cooked myself, but I don't think he was ready to believe that. Neither of us cooked the cheese that followed, obviously, though Jean-Charles had chosen the baguette that accompanied it himself with great care, making sure he got the one he considered the best specimen in the baker's shop. Fresh peaches completed the meal, and then we went out for a brief walk around the evening streets and a beer before bed.

Before bed... Bed with a bloke. I was still having trouble getting my head round this. A one-off could happen to anyone, I supposed, but here I was now, calmly preparing for a repeat performance this second night. Not just calmly preparing. Wondering at myself, I found I was actually looking forward to it...

SEVENTEEN

There was a little rain that night. It gave the morning a diamond-sharp quality. In early August, in the south, the effect was uplifting and refreshing. I had enjoyed my second night in bed with a man. Jean-Charles was quite slight in build, and so was I. I thought we were a good physical match. He'd sucked my cock in bed that night, and I'd sucked his. I'd liked that a lot. Oh dear, I thought at breakfast. I'm getting to like this a bit too much. And, oh dear, I thought again, I'm getting to like Jean-Charles too much.

I was rather afraid also that he was getting too fond of me.

'You can go back to bed if you want,' he said to me over breakfast as we finished our *biscottes* and cherry jam. 'It's only me that has to be at work at ten o'clock.'

'Well, I might stay and lounge about the house for a bit,' I said. 'I don't think I'll go back to bed, though. I'd only end up thinking about you and having a wank.'

I'd taught him that word – among a number of others. He'd taught me their equivalents in French. You never knew when they'd come in handy. The verb to wank translated into French as *branler*. Though there were several variations on that.

'Come and join me at coffee time, then,' he said. When we parted at the front door a little later he gave me a kiss. Again, oh dear, I thought.

Setting off in the newly freshened air a couple of hours later I spotted a familiar figure crossing the street. A young man wearing a football shirt and orange bell-bottoms. It was Raoul, of course. For the last twenty-four hours or more I hadn't given him a second's thought. He didn't see me, he was looking the other way. I could have called out to him, he was close enough. I was almost about to call his name, but something I suddenly noticed prevented me. I was horrified and ashamed. I realised that, from the top of his thick mane of hair, down through the striped football jersey to the bottom of his prehistoric orange flares, Raoul was soaking wet.

I told Jean-Charles about this, when I met him at the gallery a little later. 'We gave him a few francs the other night,' I said. 'And Brigitte gave him canapés and champagne. It does no real good, a little gift like that now and then.'

Jean-Charles agreed. 'It only give the giver a chance to imagine himself a better person.' A truly generous person, he went on, would have reckoned his parents' house big enough to shelter Raoul for a week or two, or would at least have made the offer. It would have cost nothing.

'That's true,' I said, 'But think of the practicalities. What would happen when your parents come back on Sunday? Even I have to go back to England then. Can you imagine your parents' reaction to finding a homeless guy had moved in?'

'You're right,' Jean-Charles said with a shake of his curls. 'It's like feeding the birds in the winter. What happens when you go away?' Then he said something I thought beautiful, though, because true, also sad. 'Few people have hearts to match the size of their apartments.'

That night while we held each other tight in bed after coming together, a storm broke. Lightning flashed as brightly into the bedroom as if the heavy curtains hadn't been there, and the thunder crashed around the sky as loudly as if the distant hills were falling down. Then came the rain, bringing down in its cacophony the whole immensity of the sky.

'Oh my God!' Jean-Charles said. 'What about poor Raoul? What's going to happen to him?' His voice trembled on the brink of tears.

'I don't know,' I said. I felt Jean-Charles's sudden emotion catch me too, and catch me out. 'We can't go out and look for him. Not in this. Not in the middle of the night. He must have experienced a storm before. He won't die.' I gave Jean-Charles a squeeze to comfort him. 'He'll be OK. And in the morning, when you go to work, I'll go and look for him. We'll take it from there. OK?'

I felt Jean-Charles's nod of reluctant acceptance as a tickle, in the darkness, of unseen blond curls. Then the lightning blazed again, the thunder split the heavens, and the big house quaked.

I spent most of the next day looking for Raoul in the streets of Arles. Shy though I was of accosting strangers in my faltering French I found myself doing just that, button-holing everyone I met who didn't look like a tourist. I walked into shops and cafés. I asked everywhere. Quite a number of people knew who I was talking about. The orange flares were a pretty distinctive identity badge, after all. I got the impression he was a popular figure in the town. Someone who did no harm, someone who wouldn't hurt a fly. Someone had seen him painting by the river once at night, with candles planted around him on the ground to light his work as he sat cross-legged on the ground, sketch-pad on knees. But no-one had seen him since the previous day.

I returned to the gallery from time to time throughout the day, reporting each time the ongoing failure of my search to Jean-Charles. At the end of the day we had dinner in a café together. Though we were more than happy in each other's company, the disappearance of Raoul had cast something over our cheerfulness. It was as if someone had thrown a towel over a bedside lampshade, or a high thin cloud were veiling the sun.

We stayed out late, though, drinking Pastis – as Van Gogh would have quaffed Absinthe, though perhaps in more moderate amounts – at the Café du Forum Then we wandered back to Jean-Charles's parents' house.

As we arrived at the front door and as Jean-Charles fumbled in his pocket for the key we practically tripped over a familiar assortment of clothes lying in a heap on the doorstep.

Jean-Charles leaned down and tried to wake Raoul with a hand on the shoulder. But he was fast asleep and unwilling to be roused. I tried another approach. I rubbed the lobe of one of his ears very gently between finger and thumb, a method I had heard of for waking people without frightening them or making them cry out – not that Raoul would have done that. It worked at once, Raoul turning a pair of calm, trusting eyes on me, and then on Jean-Charles that seemed to say, OK, now what? So Jean-Charles told him.

'You're not sleeping there tonight. This is where I live. Just come upstairs; you can sleep on my sofa. No strings. Have a shower if you want.'

Without much of a change of expression Raoul got to his feet and followed Jean-Charles through the door, while I brought up the rear. We went into the salon. 'Are you hungry?' Jean-Charles asked him. 'Do you want to eat something?'

Raoul said no with a polite smile and a wave of his fingers. It was very late after all. But the offer of a shower went down better and, once he'd been shown where it was, Raoul startled us by quite unselfconsciously taking all his clothes off in front of us, out on the landing. I might have looked away and pretended not to be interested, but I found I couldn't.

There was only so much lying to myself that I could do in one lifetime, I realised finally then, and I had done it all already. Raoul actually had a very beautiful body. It was about the same size as Jean-Charles's and my own, but softer, less wiry, and with a glowing, golden complexion that made me think bizarrely of butterscotch. He had very little hair about him: just the bare minimum that was necessary to prove that he was actually grown-up.

Once he was naked he turned towards us and smiled broadly at our state of awed suspended animation. We were awed, I think, because Raoul was sporting a full and sturdy little erection that pressed itself flat up against his belly like a teenager's and seemed to be trying to climb towards his navel in the manner of a determined but still cuddly little animal. Raoul looked around the landing quickly, then walked over to the telephone table that was there, seized a pencil and wrote something with it on the message pad. Jean-Charles and I exchanged a look of astonishment and walked over to see what Raoul had written. It was just the two words, *vous aussi*, you too, and even they were made redundant a moment later when Raoul began to undo the few buttons of our two shirts that, that hot day, had been done up in the first place.

So the three of us took our shower together, and towelled each other dry, and, all thoughts of the sofa forgotten, crept together, the three of us, into Jean-Charles's double bed and pleasured one another, not especially athletically but tenderly, comfortingly, until, arms thrown lightly across one another, we all slept.

When I awoke in the early light I didn't need to reach out a hand to know that Raoul wasn't there. I was alone with Jean-Charles in the bed. Together we got up and checked the house. The door was fastened but Raoul and all his clothes had gone. We might have thought we had jointly hallucinated the incident but for the wet bath towels and the state of the bathroom floor, and then, when we got back into bed I found I could smell the washed and youthful scent of the young man whose body had shone gold like butterscotch.

I fell into a light sleep and dreamed, for the first time in weeks, of Happy. He stood inside a lighted window that was high above me, and signalled to me to approach. I moved closer. Happy gestured to the window-pane between us. 'Break the glass,' he said.

I thought about this when I awoke again. There didn't seem much glass left to break. I'd broken the taboo I'd always carried around me about sleeping with, and having sex with, men. Last night I'd even jumped up and down on the splintered shards, it seemed to me, by sleeping with two of them at once. Where do I go from here? I had to ask myself.

I got out of bed, hearing Jean-Charles do the same on his side of the bed, and we started to dress. We were still a bit too gob-smacked by what had happened between Raoul and us to find very much to say. Then I was distracted by the sight of something shining in one of my shoes as I lifted it to put it on. The something was two ten-franc coins. I had left twenty francs in Raoul's shoes a few days ago, while he slept, and now it seemed that Raoul had done the same for me – the same two coins maybe. It was like a tip in a hotel bedroom, or a thank you for something more important than a mere night's sleep. Or – my imagination crept sideways up on this one – payment, of a sort, for sex. I smiled, and then sat down upon the bed and laughed. I'd remembered that Jean-Charles had left the same amount of money for Raoul too. He hadn't put his shoes on yet. 'What's funny?' He asked.

'Look inside your shoes,' I told him.

He looked there. *'Ah, mon dieu!'* he said.

This new day passed like the previous one. The difference was that we were both much happier. Yesterday we'd felt we'd lost Raoul somehow. Today we had the feeling that he was very much found. The long-term consequences of that might be problematic, but then the long-term consequences of anything and everything can be problematic. There was still the imminent parting of Jean-Charles and me to deal with in little more than twenty-four hours' time.

It was Saturday. I couldn't believe how quickly this week had flown. I went again to the gallery at morning coffee time. I had a request to make of Jean-Charles. 'Can I go downstairs again?' I asked him. 'I'd like to take one more look at that photo of Ian before I have to go.'

'I knew you would,' said Jean-Charles with a smile. 'Ian Smart or Ian Lewis. He's the boy you knew. I can see from your face that you've no doubt about that now.'

'I guess you're right,' I said, though I'd tried not to let myself be too certain of it up to now.

Jean-Charles asked his boss Marc to keep an eye on the door for a minute of two, and together we went down the stairs. Together we gazed at the naked youth in the dimly lit room. 'He was very beautiful,' Jean-Charles said. 'I mean, he was when I met him. He still is in the picture. No doubt he still is in real life too. As you will see when you find him again.'

'When I find him again?' I queried, startled. 'What makes you think I'm going to find him again?'

'Because you're going to look for him.' Jean-Charles looked me steadily in the eye. 'When you are back in England that is exactly what you are going to do.'

'Oh, I don't know,' I said. 'Everybody always says it's a bad idea to go looking for your past.'

'It depends what the past was, surely,' Jean-Charles said. 'If it was a good thing…'

'It wasn't a good thing,' I tried to say.

'That's what you thought at the time,' he argued. 'You were trying to save your marriage, and some ideas you had about yourself… Well, now they are all burned up behind you. That's the bad past that has gone. You should look for Ian and find happiness with him.'

Because of his French accent he made *find happiness* sound like *find a penis*. I had to smile.

I changed the subject very slightly. 'And what will become of you after I've gone? What are you going to do?'

'Oh, I don't know,' he said. 'Perhaps I will look for Raoul.'

'Come here,' I said. 'Give me a kiss.' We stood embracing in the half-dark of the basement gallery for a long, long time.

EIGHTEEN

Jean-Charles didn't have to look for Raoul that day at any rate. In the middle of that hot afternoon Raoul came to the gallery looking for… For Jean-Charles? For me? For us? Whatever the case, there he was. Jean-Charles asked him if he would have dinner with us that evening. He made it clear that Raoul would eat as his, Jean-Charles's, guest. We both watched Raoul's beautiful, impassive face as he thought about the invitation and its possible implications. This took several seconds. I felt my emotions stirred as I saw Raoul's face break into a smile, and then watched him nod his yes.

The next thing that happened was that Raoul indicated with a gesture of hand and head that he wanted to see the photos in the basement again. I was acutely conscious that it was I who would be departing from both their lives tomorrow. I wanted to be gracious in my manner of leaving the two of them. I said, 'You take him down there,' to Jean-Charles. 'I'll man the desk.'

They returned, beaming, about ten minutes later. I was more than happy to see the smiles on both their faces.

We went to the Café du Forum. The café Vincent painted in the evening, with the light spilling out from under its awning onto the terrace and the tables. When we arrived it was still daylight, and the café hadn't yet adopted its evening look. But little by little as we sat on that well-known terrace the light changed. It became the light of Van Gogh. The buildings opposite darkened as the dusk thickened, and the lights under our yellow awning came on. Lights began to glimmer at the open-shuttered windows across the street. As we drank our *soupe de pistou* and ate our duck with olives it felt as though we were inhabiting the actual canvas of Van Gogh.

I let Jean-Charles talk most. He let Raoul know that I was returning to England the next day for good. Also that his parents were returning to their house tomorrow night. He told him that he'd be a welcome guest again at home with us tonight. That he didn't need to get up and leave at the crack of dawn. His parents wouldn't be back till the evening, he repeated. After that… Well… All three of us exchanged a very expressive smile and Gallic shrugs.

I left the table at one point. I'd spotted a pay-phone on a back wall. I was pretty sure it wouldn't have been installed yet in Vincent's day. Never mind: it was today that I wanted it.

I dialled Malcolm's number in Paris. I listened to it ringing out. Saturday night, I thought glumly. Everyone goes out. I'd have to leave a message… Ring back…

But Malcolm's voice spoke. *'Allo?'*

I said simply, 'It's David. I'm passing through Paris tomorrow. Can I stay with you tomorrow night?'

'Of course you can,' Malcolm said. 'Where are you

speaking from?'

'I'm in Arles,' I said.

'Good God,' he said.

'It's a long story,' I said. 'I won't try and do it on the phone, but a hell of a lot's happened since we last spoke.' We arranged a time for me to turn up at his apartment.

I returned to the table, to find a second bottle of wine standing on top of it. 'I'm staying at Malcolm's place tomorrow night,' I said.

'That's good,' said Jean-Charles. 'Meanwhile, are you happy if Raoul sleeps again with us tonight?'

'Very happy indeed,' I said.

I fucked Raoul that night. On top of the bed. Raoul lay back and spread himself, open and inviting. Jean-Charles lent me a condom. Well, not lent me a condom. Nobody wants to be given it back afterwards. It was a free gift. I'd thought that men might be difficult to enter. But I guessed there were differences between them, as there are between everyone and everything else. Raoul was delightfully straightforward in this respect. Jean-Charles knelt on the bed, naked and erect beside us, massaging both his own and Raoul's cock.

I came all too quickly. I wasn't surprised by that. A little later, as I lay back and rested, Raoul eased his own sheathed small cock into Jean-Charles and pistonned him elegantly while I watched. I'd never have imagined previously that I'd get pleasure from watching such a scene, but I did.

And after that... Well, I couldn't be left out. Everything else had happened to me by now, or pretty much everything. This might as well be the night I lost my anal virginity. And who could I have wished to have as my deflowerer in preference to Jean-Charles? Jean-Charles with his petite and slender, unthreatening, foreskin-hooded, *bite*.

I loved every minute, and every inch, of it.

At last, after a very long time of shared sensual pleasure, we pulled the duvet up over us and, still fondling one another till the last, drifted into sleep.

We got up late, the three of us, and breakfasted together on the croissants that – fetched piping hot from the bakery by a designated family member while at home the coffee brews – form most French family's Sunday morning treat. The designated family member that day was me. There was no question, this morning, of Raoul's leaving either of us a tip.

I left in the middle of the morning, heading for the station, walking past Van Gogh's Yellow House. 'Are you sure you will be all right?' Jean-Charles asked me before I went. 'You told me it would be hard to part. As the older one of us, you knew that. And you were right, *bien sur*. Already it hurts.' It hurt for me too, of course, but I didn't tell him that. He went on, so sweetly that it made the hurt even more painful, 'I am the lucky one. I have ended up with Raoul. You are journeying on your own for a bit.'

'Even with Raoul,' I said, 'it won't be plain sailing for you. Your parents are coming back tonight…'

'That's later,' he said. 'We've got a few hours for think about that.'

'I wish you all the luck in the world,' I said.

'And you too,' he said. 'I will worry a lot.'

'No need,' I said. 'I'm a big strong boy. And we'll always keep in touch.' We held each other then, tightly, like parting lovers. *Like* parting lovers? We actually *were* parting lovers. It just happened that we'd been lovers – it had been understood between us at the outset – on a leasehold rather than a freehold basis.

Raoul joined in our au revoir embrace. On the doorstep. In full view of the street. He didn't have a stitch of clothing on him. None of us minded that.

I wasn't a big strong boy really, I discovered. On the train I cried my heart out, and not always silently, all the way to Paris.

'I lied to you,' I said. 'Lied to myself too, which is probably worse. But in the end I had to stop doing that.'

'Don't be hard on yourself,' Malcolm said. We'd gone out to a bar – one of the few that opened on Sunday evenings – opposite the stage door of the Moulin Rouge near the bottom of the rue Lepic. Henri, realising that I needed a little time alone with Malcolm, had stayed back at the apartment, preparing a supper of langoustines with garlic mayonnaise and salad, and a gateau of omelettes. It crossed my mind that if ever I was lucky enough to have a boyfriend I'd want him to be French.

I told Malcolm everything that had happened. How I'd wanted simply to question Jean-Charles about the model in the photograph but had ended up in bed and having sex with him. How I'd then gone on to sleeping with two men together on the same night. How that had cumulated with all three of us fucking one another and getting fucked by one another … I looked at my watch … within the last eighteen hours.

'Christ almighty, David,' said Malcolm. 'You don't believe in doing things by halves…'

We walked together back up the steep curved incline of the rue Lepic. I had the sensation that I was returning home to a very familiar place. And I knew that supper would be good…

The dream of Happy in the window returned again that night. 'Break the glass,' he said again. And this time my dream-self did. Just as in real life years ago, my fist sent shards and splinters flying. But unlike in real life I now stood side by side with Happy. We walked together on a pebble beach. I had no doubt now where I was. This was Dungeness, a wild expanse of shingle, pounded by waves and blasted by wind, remote from human life, remote from everywhere. I began to wake. Urgently, because I feared to let him go a second time, I seized Happy's wrists and said, 'Where? Tell me where...'

But Happy's answer cut my question off unformed. 'Look in your address book.' The shocking incongruity of the answer woke me with all the finesse of an alarm clock in a cake tin.

'And did you look in your address book?' asked Malcolm. 'Well, did you?' We were sitting in the café near the Institute where Malcolm worked. I'd put off my return to England for a day or two. I needed Malcolm to talk things through with. I needed to sort myself out. The day's work was over for Malcolm and there was a small beer in front of both of us.

'Did I look in my address book? No, of course not!' The question made me laugh. 'I wouldn't expect the promptings of the unconscious to be so crudely literal,' I said.

'Maybe that was your problem all along,' said Malcolm.

I gave him a look. 'I do not believe, and never have,

that dreams have any prophetic or guiding power.'

Malcolm slowly turned the stem of his beer glass. 'But they do come from the subconscious, you'd agree with that. And that in that case they might do a useful job, just occasionally, in reminding us of things that are important but which our conscious memories have forgotten. Either by accident or...' He hesitated, but then finished the thought anyway. '...Or deliberately buried.'

I knew full well that Happy's address had never found its way between the pages of my address book but nevertheless, since I'd brought the thing to France with me, in one of the side pockets of my backpack, that night I looked.

Malcolm, at breakfast, was exasperated. 'Well, do it now! Ring the bloody number. Use the phone here. We won't listen in.'

'It's just a coincidence, that's all,' I said. 'Both surnames beginning with L. I'd never thought about it before. I always knew Ian's parents' number was on that page; it's no big deal.'

'Yes, but not that London number pencilled in. Where did that come from?'

'From that ex-classmate of his I met a year ago, I guess. I really don't remember.'

'Erased from the mind but not from your phone book.

What an awesome thing the pencil is.' And Malcolm bullied me until I phoned.

I returned to the breakfast table. 'Moved last Christmas,' I said. 'So that's that.'

'You are incredible, David. Don't tell me they didn't give you a new number for him.'

'Well, they did actually, but...'

'Then go ring it!'

'Maybe when I'm back in England tomorrow,' I said. I wasn't returning across the Channel today. Malcolm had arranged for me to have an interview with his boss at the Institute. 'But hell,' I said, 'I don't know why I'd want to do that. It'd only be to say hello.'

'Ring it.'

I did. Ian had moved again, a pleasant voice informed me. Someone in the flat who was out at present would have the number. Could he ring back? He rang back. It was all more complicated than that, a new voice told him. Ian had moved again. I was given the number of someone who might possibly know where.

As the task grew more frustrating so, paradoxically, I began to warm to it and Malcolm's urging was reduced to a mere background hum. The pursuit for its own sake was becoming more interesting than its object which was, after all, only to say hello.

It took two days. On each of those days I had an

interview with someone at Malcolm's place of work. It seemed as though, provided I qualified on the course I was planning to do in London, and got my certificate, I could expect to come here and get a teaching job. But apart from going to those interviews I had little to do. I might as well spend my time making useless phone-calls, I thought. And so I did. But then at last the telephone gave me a voice there was no mistaking. It was my own physical reaction to it that surprised me. Afraid of what my voice might do, I hesitated before saying, 'It's David here. I rang to say hello.'

The silence from the other end seemed as if it would last for ever. Anxiously, all too anxiously, I broke it myself, my voice finally betraying me. 'Ian, are you still there?'

'Yes,' came back firmly from the other end. Then more softly, 'I always was.'

NINETEEN

We arranged to meet at the Sun in Splendour, at the bottom end of the Portobello Road. I had been away from London for little more than a week. But the shock of that return! It wasn't that London had changed a lot in the intervening days. All the change was in me.

Ian had only to walk for twenty minutes to get to the Sun in Splendour. He lived in a shared flat near Powis Square. I made the pilgrimage by tube. I was staying with a group of friends of mine, singles of both sexes, who also shared a flat, but in Stockwell, south of the Thames. They had sheltered me, in between my travels, quite a lot during the past year.

And so I found myself walking up the steps, and then the road, from Notting Hill Gate tube station to the corner where the pub stood, its unique bowed frontage following the curve of the pavement between Pembroke Road and the Portobello. I took a nervous breath and opened the door.

I'd known the Sun in Splendour well in earlier days. I hadn't set foot inside it for years, but I still knew its layout well enough to know that what I could see was what there was. And what there wasn't… Ian wasn't there.

At least he wasn't there yet. The rules of chivalry dictate that when a guy arranges to meet a lone woman in a pub he shall arrive early, so as not to expose a lady to the awkwardness of waiting among strangers on her own. I wondered now how this played out among gay men. Was the senior one supposed to arrive first? If so, it seemed I'd obeyed the rule.

Now what would I have to drink? What would Ian drink these days? I had no idea. It was nearly two years since we'd seen each other. Then he'd been a boy of seventeen. Now he would be nineteen, and a man. A world-full of life and experience, of change and adventure had been his in the meantime. I had no idea who or what I had arranged to meet this early evening. Though neither, of course, had he…

The door opened and in he came.

He'd grown.

When we'd last we met he'd been about the same height as I was. Now he was about two inches taller. He was better muscled than me, now, though only just. He was beautiful. The photograph I'd seen of him in Arles, taken a year ago, was beautiful. I had no doubt at all now that he was the boy in the picture. But the way he looked this evening was something else. I found I wanted to say everything all at once. I didn't. I said, 'Ian, it's good to see you.' I held out my hand and we shook.

'Good to see you too,' Ian said, very adult, very cool.

We couldn't go on like this. I said, 'Ian, is it OK if I give you a hug?'

A hug is a very revealing thing. It's like a

thermometer. Tells you what you need to know in the space of a minute. Or less. Ian's hug told me that he was OK about hugging me, but only just. My hug told him – told both of us – that suddenly, unexpectedly, I'd realised I wanted him very much. There was a degree of mismatch between where we were each at.

'I don't know what you drink these days,' I heard myself saying. 'Tell me what you'd like.' He chose a pint of Stella and I ordered the same thing for myself. We looked around for a vacant table. There wasn't one, but a second later a couple got up and left one and, as if executing a joint Rugby tackle, we dived for it and grabbed it round the legs before anyone else could.

'Why did you get in touch?' Ian asked me as soon as we'd said Cheers.

I said, 'Because I wanted to. Because I like you. There's a long story behind that, but it'll keep. Are you OK with that to be going on with?'

He nodded. 'How is Anne?' he asked. He was a smart kid.

'I think she's fine,' I said. 'There's a new man in her life. We got divorced. Did you know that?'

He winced slightly. 'I'm not sure if I knew it or if I sort of guessed.' Oh, he knew all right.

There was a hiatus during which we found it difficult to look at each other. I glimpsed his blue eyes through his long dark lashes. I saw them remembering his hurt.

He spoke. 'We fucked each other up.' A sentence that tore into me like a knife.

I was the older one by nine years. It was for me to deal with this. 'For any hurt I've done you … I'm deeply sorry. It's a hopeless word, an inadequate word, but it's the only one there is. Any hurt I've suffered – if I have – I've inflicted on myself. There's nothing in anything that happened that was your fault.'

'I'm sorry anyway,' he said.

'I love you, Ian,' I almost said. And then I was horrified at myself.

I found myself smiling at him. 'Would you agree with me that we don't need to discuss that right this minute? That we might want to meet again another time? And that for the moment we could just enjoy each other's company for an hour and chill out?'

He rewarded me with a flash of eyes and a smile that became a laugh. In that moment he became again the teenager I'd known for years, the boy I'd watched grow up. Just for a second it was as though nothing had happened in between those days and now; it was as though we'd never been apart. I said, 'Tell me what you've been doing with yourself this week?'

We talked for an hour. We talked about small things, not big ones. Perhaps that was wise of us. At one point I asked him, because I genuinely couldn't remember, if he was a fan of Van Gogh. 'A bit of one, perhaps,' he said. Then he astonished me. He said, 'I know that Happy was.'

'You knew that?' I didn't know he'd even heard of Happy, let alone that he knew that about him. 'Did I tell you about Happy? I don't remember doing that.'

'You didn't,' Ian said. 'Anne did.'

'Oh,' I said. We eyeballed each other across the table for a moment. Oh dear. How lovely he looked.

'She told me how upset you'd been about his death. I think she thought that you…' He shook his head with a jolt, as if his train of thought had hit a rough patch of track. 'No, forget that.' He started to talk about something else.

I hadn't known how or when our meeting would wind up. I'd left that to him deliberately. I wanted him to handle it his way, and so he did. He looked at his watch. 'I'd better go,' he said. 'We're eating in tonight and it's sort of my turn to cook.'

I took this on the chin, or at least pretended I did. 'Fair enough,' I said. 'It's been lovely seeing you.'

'It was good to see you too,' he said, and his eyes dropped, so that I got a view simply of his long lashes.

I was very calm as I said, feeling my way with this, like an angler reeling in a fish that he has only very lightly hooked, 'I wonder if I might buy you dinner one night next week. Would you be OK with that?'

He didn't meet my gaze. Not yet. I had the feeling he was speaking from behind the shelter of his eyelashes as he said quietly, 'Yes, I'd like that.'

I was tempted to try and nail an evening there and then. Something told me not to do that. I took a bigger risk. For much higher stakes. 'Can I phone you in a day or two?' I asked. 'Then we can fix a day.' I just managed not to say date. 'Is that all right?' He said it was.

We stood up then and walked out into the street. His way lay leftward, mine to the right. We embraced momentarily on the pavement. It's funny how you always know whether there is or isn't going to be a kiss. We knew there wasn't going to be. Not tonight.

As I walked away, resisting the almost overpowering urge to turn round and look back, I thought at once of all the big questions we hadn't asked. Neither of us had said, are you in a relationship? Neither of us had volunteered the answer to that. He hadn't asked me if I was gay. Though I wouldn't have expected him to. I was nine years older than him and had been a married man when we'd last met. He on the other hand had declared his love for me drunkenly when he was seventeen. He might well have spent the intervening years feeling painfully foolish about that. It was good of him to agree to meet me, in the circumstances.

And yet… That first exchange of words of ours on the telephone a fortnight back was etched on my memory. I even remembered exactly his tone of voice. Are you still there? I'd asked him. Yes, he'd said. *I always was.*

I hadn't asked him if he was gay either. Not yet. Give him space, I thought. Give him time and space. I heard my breath come out as a large loud sigh as I reached the top of the steps at Notting Hill Gate. So great a sigh, so painful a heave. It was nearly a sob.

I tried a T-shirt on and turned in front of the mirror, this way and that. It looked too obvious that I was trying to age down, to take away those nine years that lay between us, that always had done, that always would. I replaced it with various open-necked shirts, one after another, then took them off. I spent over half an hour in front of the mirror that evening. It was the kind of thing Anne used to do – and she wasn't alone among womankind in that. I used to tease her about it, as most husbands do. But as for me, I had never done such a thing before in my life.

In the end I chose a plain white collarless linen shirt. Then I agonised over how many buttons I should leave undone. Just two? Or three? Or - *four?* Bloody hell, mate, I told myself... I knew that my chest looked good however much or little of it I might expose. But that was not the point... I settled for three in the end. It was a hot night. I didn't bother with a jacket. I just jammed everything into my jeans pockets and went out.

We met in the Sun in Splendour as before. I was

happy to see Ian looking much more relaxed tonight. That made me relax too, and I saw Ian clock that. I also saw that he'd taken some trouble, just as I had, to look his best. I found myself surprisingly, and deeply, moved by that.

At my suggestion we had a gin and tonic this time. A large one. I was paying, after all. I'd had my experiences of going to restaurants after several pints of beer and then having to keep leaving the table during dinner to let the water out. I didn't want either of us to have to deal with that particular embarrassment tonight. If we ever got to know each other better, then maybe that would be all right. We weren't at that stage yet...

We walked together across Notting Hill Gate and into Hillgate Street, where there was a small Italian restaurant I'd known for years. It was home territory, and I felt safe.

When we were seated I returned to the subject of Van Gogh. I'd now had plenty of time to rehearse this scene: I wanted to try and get it right. I told him how a friend had invited me to go to Provence with him, with a view to helping me get over the trauma of my divorce. How he'd been a Van Gogh freak, just as Happy had, and had taken me on his track. I saw his ears prick slightly at the mention of Provence. I now said, 'We went to Arles...'

He almost gave a start. I pressed on. 'I saw something very beautiful there in an art gallery.'

'Oh,' he said. 'What was that?'

'I just wondered,' I said, 'if you might guess.'

He looked cross for a second. 'Don't tease me,' he said.

'I won't,' I said. 'But if I get this wrong I'm going to be hideously embarrassed. OK, I'll tread carefully. I saw a photo of a young man on a river bank.'

This time he really did start; he couldn't disguise it. I smiled, trying to relax him, wanting to show him I was OK about it. 'A very nice looking young man, naked. I might be wrong, and if I am, that's the embarrassing bit…'

He didn't let me go on struggling. Bless his lovely heart. 'You were right. It was me,' he said.

'I'm very glad of that,' I said, and we both laughed. With a sound like breaking ice, or breaking glass.

I had to tell him, because he was curious, about how I'd met Jean-Charles and his boss. I didn't tell him I'd had sex with him – let alone had a threesome with him and Raoul. There might one day be a time and place for telling everything, but this was certainly not it.

I changed the subject. I told Ian I was going to do a short course in teaching English as a foreign language. 'My friend Malcolm introduced me to the bosses of the business school he works at in Paris,' I said. I adopted an expression, or tried to, that would convey the idea of *Qué será, será*. 'See what happens,' I said. 'It's one option. I haven't decided yet.'

Ian wasn't going to go down on his knees and beg me not to go to Paris but to stay with him in London. He wasn't going to tell me he'd rather I got a job washing dishes in this very Italian restaurant than move three hundred miles away across the sea. And of course he didn't.

It wasn't until that very moment, though, that I discovered I wished he would.

A young Italian was playing a guitar in one corner of the small space. As we came towards the end of our meal two young couples at a nearby table got up and started to dance. It was brave of them: the space was extremely cramped. After two dances they called it a day, vanquished by that constraint. They began to sit down again, and the two girls actually did. But the boys did not. Halfway to sitting down they seemed to change their minds – jointly. They both got up again.

They were back on the dance floor together. On was Italian, the other English, I guessed. They held each other, their cheeks so close they could have leaned in easily for a kiss. But then the Italian one turned aside to speak to the guitarist. 'Play 'Feelings',' he said. And the guitarist did.

To say the two boys danced together would be overstating it. Their feet didn't leave the floor. But they held each other, swaying with the music, with the unmistakeable intimacy of two people who – even if they don't actually love each other - are deeply attracted and closely attached. They were two people who – even if they didn't know this consciously – would at some level have liked to have sex.

The dance didn't last more than a few seconds. The boys broke apart, their faces expressing both disappointment and awkwardness. Frustration too perhaps. The guitarist's accompaniment petered out. The men joined their girlfriends - or wives - back at the table. Ian and I looked at each other. To say the looks we exchanged at that moment were heavily freighted would have been a major understatement.

One of us had to speak. I found it was me. 'When I was in Provence,' I said, 'I made more than just one discovery. Among other things I discovered was the fact that I'm gay.' I adapted Ian's own phrase. 'I probably always was.'

In a very small and diffident voice, almost a whisper, Ian said, 'I'm gay too. I probably always was.'

TWENTY

At one time I thought that being gay – if you were – was about the biggest thing you could find you had in common with a fellow human being. That it was the biggest bond you could have. I was wrong. It isn't. It's quite a small thing actually. Think of it the other way round. Two guys are heterosexual… Automatic bond between them? I think not.

So we didn't rush into each other's arms across the restaurant table. We didn't go to bed together that night. But we parted friends. Rather good friends. There was a bond of understanding between us. There was affection. And we'd told each other we were gay. All right, it wasn't a big thing. But it wasn't nothing.

A week after that I became enormously busy. My training course began. I thought it would be easy. I'd been teaching English for years, after all. But it was far from that. Our trainers made a point of smashing to pieces all the assumptions I had about teaching. I saw what they were about. They needed to rebuild me, as a teacher, from scratch. It was a very different kind of teaching I was about to do. Instead of English school-kids with whom I shared a language, a culture and a load of assumptions and other baggage, I would be working with adults with whom I shared none of the above. It was pointed out to me, as one example, that while the word dog evokes up a warm cuddly feeling in British people, for people in many countries it conjures up primeval fears, of the jungle, of the lawless, rabid, scavenged back streets. I could make no assumptions about even the things I thought of as basic.

I had a lot to learn. They made me learn it. Because I'd been a teacher – I was the only specimen in my group of fifteen – they often picked on me in front of the whole class, to make an example. To rub home the fact that what we were learning to do was nothing like we'd experienced at school. I didn't like it. I bore it. I didn't let it get me down, although it might easily have done had there been no-one in my life. What buoyed me up was … Ian.

At the end of the day I would phone him up and we'd have a chat. He'd tell me his daily woes. About his English degree course at UCL. I'd tell him my about my tribulations too. Once a week we'd meet for a drink or dinner. Once I went to his flat. Once he came to mine. We enjoyed each other's company. That was as far as it went.

'Are you still planning to go to Paris?' he asked me more than once.

Please ask me not to go, a voice inside me begged. *Tell me you need me. Ask me to stay and I'll do that. I'll get a job here in London washing dishes. Just say one word.* The outward me said, 'Probably. I'm still not sure, though. Do you have a better idea?' He did not. *Just say the word.* But he did not.

If I was going to work in Paris I would need somewhere to live. I couldn't stay in Malcolm and Henri's small spare room for ever. Through a friend they found me what they called a *chambre de bonne*. It meant a maid's room, an attic bedroom in effect. The mansard roofs of the Paris skyline were crammed with these. The maids had long gone, and their empty nest-holes had been for the most part converted into small studio flats, inhabited by students and the likes of me – single young workers who were not yet rich.

My four-week intensive (extremely intensive!) course finished. A week later I got my results. I got a grudging pass. But a pass is still a pass, as time goes by, and the grudge fades into meaninglessness.

Still, I would have cancelled everything, and risked the wrath of Malcolm's employers had Ian said or done anything to stop me at the last moment. But still he didn't. We had a farewell dinner together. I said, 'You promise you'll come and spend a weekend with me in Paris as soon as I'm settled?'

He said, 'I will.' Then he smiled beautifully at me across the table. It was far from being a marriage vow but it was the best I was going to get.

I didn't ask him to come with me to the airport. That would have been too cruel to both of us. Instead I went on my own. Van Gogh had left London, all alone, for

Paris in March 1896 – I was following him in September 1989. The parallel was not exact. A neat centenary would have been pleasing, but never mind.

Van Gogh had travelled by ship. There was no other way, back then. Unlike Vincent I had a choice. I went with Air France, taking off from Heathrow just before four o'clock. I wondered what, if any, refreshments would be provided by the French flag-carrier during the forty-minute hop. It turned out to be a quarter-bottle of Moët et Chandon, red-sealed and gold-foil-wrapped, placed without fuss on every seat-back table as we crossed the French coast overhead the docks of Dieppe. I had to hand it to them. Nobody has style like the French.

Things don't always go like clockwork, though. The Institute wanted me to start on a Monday, naturally, while my studio wouldn't be ready until two days after that. Nor was Malcolm able to put me up. He was away with Henri for those few days, and Malcolm's brother and his sister-in-law were staying in the flat in rue Lepic. I checked into a cheap hotel at La Motte-Piquet.

And then I began my new life.

I had ordered breakfast for seven-thirty. It was served to me and to half a dozen twitching travelling salesmen by a pale Pole who doubled as a night porter as he passed bleary nights studying economics text-books in French. There was coffee in bowls, and baguettes cut in chunks to dunk in it. There were no croissants at seven-thirty on a Monday.

It took me exactly twelve minutes to walk to the Institute. The wind took my old Durham Castle scarf and wrapped it twice around my throat as if it meant to strangle me with my own umbilicus before I could snatch even my first breath of this new life. Then, as I crossed the threshold of my new place of work it occurred to me that existing in a new language was going to involve a marathon repetition of firsts. That first day at school – an event as impossible to repeat, I'd thought, as the death of a hero – now had to be undergone again, this time in French. So it would be with the first visit to the doctor, to the hairdresser; with the first altercation, with the hesitations of the first new intimacy, the sorrow of the first parting. Only in English were these rites of passage behind me and unrepeatable. I realised now that my relative unfamiliarity with the language would leave me as fragile and unprotected an arrival in this francophone world as a newborn child. The door shut behind me and I began once again my first day at school.

There had been two first times in my case, of course. On the first occasion I was five. My mother had towed me by the arm down the slope to the entrance, uncoupled with difficulty my tightening fingers from her own and hooked them into another hand which belonged, I soon discovered, not to a woman or man but to a new thing called a teacher. It was not a happy morning and everyone had cried, including me. The second time I hadn't cried, though

I'd felt just the same, but that time I'd been twenty-two and myself a new thing called a teacher.

'Monsieur Walton?' said the receptionist, pricking up her ears as I announced my name. *'Vous avez un groupe à neuf heures.'* I had a group at nine o'clock, apparently. It was now eight fifty.

'Ce n'est pas possible,' I said, trying not to let my panic be heard in my voice. I had nothing prepared. Really, this third round in the David versus School contest was going to be as bad as the others. 'Madame Suger told me that my first class would be a one-to-one this afternoon. I came in early just to see where things are and to prepare for later on.' This speech sounded less impressive in my halting French.

The director of studies, sailing into the reception area just then, came to my rescue, or so I thought. She was a tall, elegant Englishwoman who had been trying out Parisian chic for twenty years and had very nearly got the hang of it. 'You're David, aren't you?' she said, smiling. 'I'm Rebecca.' She offered varnished nails. I tweaked them nervously. 'Madame Suger told me about you. Now this class at nine o'clock. We can't possibly expect you to do it, of course.' Her smile widened reassuringly. 'Not at zero notice. It isn't on your programme and you've only just arrived.' I nodded with gratitude and relief. 'On the other hand...' The smile vanished and she gave me a penetrating look through fashionable spectacles. 'We've got two teachers sick this morning and we'd be ever so grateful if you could ... at least, just till eleven o'clock. By then I'll have found someone else to hang in till lunchtime. You'd still have time to prepare for the afternoon.'

'But...'

'They've got books.' Rebecca had played this scene before. 'At least I think they have. It's *Salle Numéro Sept.*'

Faced with the choice between accepting and refusing additional work on your first morning, what did you do? I'd found himself rapidly and expertly manoeuvred beyond choice or decision. Within five minutes I was in *Classroom Number Seven*, teaching English to a computer programmer, an air hostess, a journalist, an accountant and two secretaries and trying, as Rebecca had advised, to *make it relevant.*

'How much are they paying you?'

'Pardon?'

'How much are they paying you?' The question came from under thatched eaves of hair, well coiffed but designed to leave the face beneath a shadowy, enigmatic affair. The voice and hairstyle belonged to a small, mouse-like woman who was seated at the staffroom table. Other people, preparing lessons as I was, had left me temporarily *à deux* with this stranger who had not responded when I'd introduced myself to the room in general. 'Well, how much?'

'The normal rate, I suppose,' I said. 'Like everyone else.'

'Don't you believe it,' said the voice under the thatch. 'There isn't a normal rate. We're all paid differently. You wouldn't credit it, would you? But it's true.' The woman's face now seemed to be peering out of a burrow, nose a-twitch and small eyes darting. 'They do it so that none of us can trust one another. It stops us from getting together to improve things.'

'I suppose it would do,' I said blandly.

'It's disgraceful,' the other went on. 'Do you know, we're not allowed to join a *syndicat*?'

'What's a *syndicat*?' I asked, though I could guess.

'A trade union,' the woman said. 'I don't know why we put up with it. You ought to do something, you know.'

'Me?'

'Strike while the iron's hot,' said the woman in an impassioned squeak. 'You had to do an extra class this morning without notice. You shouldn't let them get away with that. They'll be walking over you in no time.'

'It's still only my first day.' I wasn't sure whether to be alarmed or amused. 'It might be just a bit soon to proclaim the revolution. I mean, coming from me. How long have you been here?'

'Twelve years. I don't know why. They don't thank

you. They don't appreciate loyalty.' She lowered her voice to a rustle. 'This hell hole, it's run by a coven of witches. Did you know that?'

To my relief two other people came in, talking together, and my own conversation ended. I buried my head unnecessarily deeply in a text-book until it was time for lunch.

The afternoon's one-to-one lesson presented me with a large, jowly man who faced me across a table and informed me, 'I don't want grammar or exercises; I want to talk.'

I closed the text-book. 'OK. We'll talk.' And my student turned out to be as taciturn an individual as I'd ever passed an afternoon with, while my watch crept towards five o'clock like a train passing a succession of signals set at amber.

It was a delicious novelty to finish a day's work and to be at the same time in a foreign country. Today, for the first time in my life, I found that I could step abroad and into all its associations just by stopping my class on time and walking out into the street.

Near at hand a bright shop window displayed charcuterie, champagne and those jewel-like hors d'oeuvres of eggs and seafood set in aspic. All up the street other lighted windows gave promise of the same and more. At the end of the vista one giant leg of the Eiffel Tower appeared, framed by the surrounding buildings. It seemed to be stepping on stage teasingly, like a showgirl: this glimpse of leg a coquettish preliminary to the grand entrance the Tower would make if I would only cross the road and move towards it. I did cross the road. I'd seen a phone-box. I went into it and phoned Ian. We talked for ages, and when I put the phone down I felt that all was well again with the world.

TWENTY-ONE

Two days later I moved into my bright-windowed apartment under the zinc roof of an *immeuble* just off the Place Blanche. The little square lay at the bottom of the rue Lepic, and was just five minutes' walk from Malcolm's flat. Even better, by now Malcolm was back.

We met for the first time at the end of the day's work. There was so much I wanted to tell him. He forestalled me. 'Let's go for a beer,' he said. 'There's a café round the corner the others don't use. Then we can talk.'

And talk I did. I told him all about Ian. About where we'd got to. About where we had not. 'The trouble is, I've rather fallen for him,' I ended up.

Malcolm said, with a little laugh, 'Oh, I knew you'd do that.' Then, 'When are you seeing him next?'

'I've asked him to come to Paris once I've settled,'

'Ah,' he said, nodding wisely. 'I wouldn't leave it as long as that.'

'I'll bear that advice in mind,' I said. 'I phone him every evening anyway. I'll be phoning him later tonight.'

'Good,' Malcolm said. 'I'm glad to hear that.' Then he changed the subject, and we began to talk about the place, a mere two hundred metres away, where we worked. 'What did you have today?' he asked.

'A four-hour intensive group in the morning and a one-to-one in the afternoon,' I told him. 'And you?' I asked.

'About the same,' Malcolm said. 'Except my morning was 'in-company'. That's quite good. It means you spend some of your time riding around Paris on buses and trains and things. When you're new it helps you get to know the city and when you're not it serves to remind you that it's all still out there – Paris I mean – looking beautiful. When you work in a place like this for a while it's dead easy to forget that. And you can do your lesson prep on the bus as well if you get tired of sightseeing. Mind you, they won't let you loose on the company classes for a month or two. You'll have to stay here under Madame Suger's petticoats a while yet. Till they feel sure they can trust you. Have you had any problems with Sarah today?'

'Who's Sarah?' I asked. Then I guessed. 'Is she the woman who looks like a mouse peering out of a thatched roof?'

'Got her in one,' Malcolm said.

I had indeed had a run-in with the thatched woman earlier that day. There had been an electric heater in my classroom which I'd switched on a while before my morning lesson. Returning to the room a few minutes later with a book I'd forgotten, I'd caught Sarah in the act of removing my heater in order to install it in her own room next door. I had already noticed that her room had its own heater. 'I feel the cold more than other people,' she'd claimed when I protested. An unseemly argument had ensued in front of the students, taboo among teachers everywhere, which had only ended when I physically wrested the heater from Sarah's grasp, winning not through any persuasive power but mere male might. I still felt rather bad about this.

'She's a witch,' Malcolm said matter-of-factly when I'd finished the tale. 'I guessed you might have trouble with her. That's why I asked. Who else have you met?'

I'd met two American guys who were very different from each other. 'I've met George,' I said. 'And I've met Huck.'

'Ah,' said Malcolm. 'George first. Well, he crossed the Atlantic to forget his divorced wife and her kids. Now do you know Katie?'

'Haven't met her yet. But don't tell me. She came here to forget her husband. Right?'

'That's not the half of it. George was the husband she came to forget. And here he was in Paris, working at the same school. God, I'd like to have been a fly on the wall when they first met up in the *salle des profs*. It's a small world, I know, but George and Katie couldn't have guessed it was quite that small. Now Huck. He came all the way from New York to forget he was positive.'

'Positive?'

'HIV. He seems to think that now he's in Paris it'll

sort of go away. Dear, lovely Huck\. I mean I know Paris has its magic but there are limits…'

Later I phoned Ian and we chatted. Our chats got a little longer each night, I was noticing. I liked that. I just hoped he didn't feel the opposite. I jumped in now with both feet. 'Can you come to Paris this weekend?' I invited. 'I'd pay your fare, of course. I'd really like that.' I heard my voice falter as I added, 'If you would…'

There was a moment's silence. It was long enough to give my heart time to sink. Then I heard Ian say, 'I can't do this weekend. It's too short notice. I've got coursework. Or the next one. But I could do the one after that. Would that be all right?'

My heart leapt and sang and capered. 'It would be wonderful,' I said. I couldn't say less than that.

And then I caught up with Malcolm again, and had supper with him and Henri in their apartment in the rue Lepic. We sat in the salon, surrounded by Vincent's golden fields of wheat and sunflowers. I told them the news about Ian's forthcoming visit, and they said well done, and drank my health.

I walked back to the Place Blanche with my heart full of light.

The phone rang just after eight. It was Rebecca, the

director of studies. I could feel the clutch of her varnished nails through the bedclothes. 'I know you're not due to teach before two o'clock,' Rebecca said, 'but could you, exceptionally, cover a class from nine-thirty till twelve-thirty? I've got someone to hold it for the first hour.'

'I'm in bed,' I protested.

'Would you be able to make it for nine-thirty?' Rebecca said.

I felt the nails digging in. After a tiny pause, the voice on the phone – now modulated into a more sombre key – added, 'You know we'll always try to accommodate teachers when they have their own timetable problems. These things have to work two ways, I feel, or not at all.'

I had felt the nails meet, somewhere just below my diaphragm. 'All right,' I said. The class I found myself teaching, a rushed hour later, was in a bad humour, its equilibrium upset by the non-appearance of its usual teacher. I struggled to kindle in the group some enthusiasm for gerunds and infinitives, but finished the lesson wishing – at one with the students for the first time that morning – that I hadn't bothered. The afternoon passed only marginally more happily and it came as a great relief at five o'clock to step out into the street and watch the Eiffel Tower do likewise as I crossed the road towards the café. I'd arranged to meet Malcolm there in fifteen minutes.

We'd met at lunchtime already, though. He had asked me, out of the blue, 'How are you getting on with *la Sorcière*?'

'With what?'

'Sarah. Have you thrown any more heaters at each other?'

'Heaters, no,' I said. 'We had a set-to over the photocopier, though. She decided she had the right to jump the queue because she only had four copies to make and had arrived late for her class into the bargain.'

'Trying it on. Did you let her?'

I laughed. 'Hell I did. I took the opportunity to do some of my copying for tomorrow as well while I was in front of her. She was pretty livid but there wasn't much she could do. On the other hand she had the gall to ask me for five francs during the coffee break, saying she had no change for the coffee machine – which only requires two francs anyway.'

Malcolm chuckled. 'That's our Sarah.' We'd gone on to talk of other things.

I reached the café now and went inside. I ordered myself a *panaché*, a shandy, and at the same moment, to my great surprise, Sarah entered. *La Sorcière*. She was wearing dark glasses, which gave her the conspicuous appearance of someone who did not want to be recognized – and made her all the more conspicuous since we were indoors and the café was not particularly brightly lit. The effect in combination with her thatch--like coiffure was striking. But if the dark glasses, like the hair, made it impossible for outsiders to peer in, they apparently didn't diminish her own ability to see out. She made straight for me and said, 'There you are. I thought I'd find you here.'

I didn't feel under any obligation to be courteous. 'I was hoping to see Malcolm,' I said. 'And now you're looking for me. Must be my lucky day.'

For answer Sarah opened her purse, took out a five-franc coin and rapped it smartly on the counter like a small hammer. 'I owe you that,' she said. 'From this morning.'

I said, 'You haven't come here specially to give me five francs.'

She turned black lenses on me. She might have been looking searchingly into my eyes. On the other hand her own might have been shut. 'No,' she said. 'I'd like you to order me a Côtes du Rhône.'

I laughed. Finally, when people were so preposterous, that was all there was to do. When I ordered the drink it arrived at once. In France that was one of the additional benefits to be derived from female company – even, it now appeared, from Sarah's.

'There's going to be a *Comité d'Entreprise*,' she announced after a small sip of wine. She had said neither cheers nor thank you.

'A what?'

'I'll explain. Every company over a certain size has one. Ours has just reached that size. Due, in actual fact, to your recent arrival. You appear to have hit the jackpot. That or been the last straw.'

'You don't make yourself clear at all,' I said. 'What is this committee?'

'The *Comité d'Entreprise* is a social committee that'll organise things like cheap theatre tickets, painting classes, staff outings...'

'Ouch,' I said.

'Staff outings not your *tasse de thé*? No, I was fairly sure they wouldn't be. But that's actually not what I came to talk about.'

'So...?'

'Along with the *comité* they want two *délégués du personnel* and if your French isn't up to understanding what that means I'll spell it out. A *délégué du personnel* represents the staff to the management – in the case of a dispute about pay, for example; conditions of employment, contracts and so on.' She switched her attention away from me, rapped another coin on the counter and called for change for some purpose which I couldn't catch, so rapid was her French.

'In other words they want two poor sods to stick their necks out,' I summed up. 'Who's standing?'

'No-one so far. The list of names for the *Comité d'Entreprise* is full, but the other one next to it is conspicuously empty. – *Ah, merci.*' Her change had arrived.

'I can't say I'm surprised,' I said. 'Madame Suger and Rebecca together would make a formidable pair of opponents at the negotiating table, I imagine. At the table and beyond.'

'Exactly. For that reason I think we should stand.'

'We?'

'Yes, David. We. I mean you and I.'

'What in the world has put this idea into your head? You hardly know me from Adam and in any case I've only just arrived. I've hardly got to grips with the language lab. let alone anything else.'

'It doesn't matter. I already have you taped, marked out, or whatever you like to call it these days. We are the best two people for those jobs, like it or not, whether you like the idea of working with me or not. Someone has to do it. It needs doing.'

'OK, but why me? You may have your own reasons for wanting to do it; for all I know you'll do a good job. But don't go including me in your plans. Why not ask one of the others? I plucked two names at random from among the colleagues I'd already met. What about George, or Huck?' I was regretting my choice of a *panaché* rather than something stronger.

'George is an oaf, as you must have noticed already,' she answered, 'and Huck isn't as strong as we'd all like him to be; you must know that too. But I think you may have a gift, Peter, as a builder of bridges, an ironer-out of creases. I see it in your face, in the way you talk. As the French say, *tu sais mettre les choses à plat.* '

'Good God,' I said. I wondered if perhaps Sarah really was a witch, or in some way clairvoyant. 'OK, but compliments apart, I don't know anything about French employment legislation, company law or anything like that. I'd be quite useless.'

'Ah yes, but in that respect I would not be,' Sarah said. 'I worked once in a French law firm. It was a long time ago, I must admit – fifteen years or more. But I still know where to get my hands on the bits of paper. That's where I come in. Also, I have a portable typewriter. We'd complement each other. You're good at handling people, which I'm not.'

'You're asking me to put my head on a block, you realize that.'

'Someone has to.'

'And get it chopped off?'

'The clever ones don't.'

'Supposing I'm not clever.'

'Supposing you are. Just say yes. Go on.'

'I'll think about it.'

'Bloody hell!' Sarah exploded. Other people turned to look. She lowered her voice to a hiss. 'People who say they'll think about things always find an excuse not to do them. Just say yes. Say it.' She took off her dark glasses and pushed the hair back from her eyes. They were the same beady brown ones I remembered but now they seemed to indicate that they might be ready to smile if certain conditions were met. 'Also, I suspect,' she said, 'there's someone in your life you'd like to try and impress.'

'Dear God!' I said. 'Where did you get that idea from?'

She shrugged and smiled. 'Just a hunch,' she said. 'Woman's intuition, if you like.'

'Merde,' I said. 'I'll do it. You're on. All right?'

'I didn't really doubt that you'd say yes,' said Sarah. 'I feel I know you quite well, though we've scarcely met.'

Wait till I tell Ian this! I thought. How uncannily Sarah had hit that last nail on the head. That I wanted to impress Ian. Of course I did.

Our *tête-à-tête* ended then. The door opened and Malcolm came in. His eyebrows rose in surprise as he saw the two of us.

TWENTY-TWO

'That was a shock,' Malcolm said, after Sarah had finished her glass of Côtes du Rhone and left. Though she'd stayed long enough for the new development to be discussed between the three of us. 'But it'll probably do you good. Stop you moping over Ian for a bit.'

'I'm not moping over Ian,' I said. 'You forget, he's coming here in less than three weeks.'

'I hadn't forgotten,' Malcolm said. 'But you're still moping over him. And after he's spent a weekend here with you and has gone back to London again, you'll be moping even worse.'

'We'll cross that bridge when we come to it,' I said.

'Anyway,' said Malcolm, evidently deciding to lighten things a bit, 'it'll give you something to brag to him about. Even if, in the end, it costs you your job.'

'Thanks a bunch,' I said.

During my first week as a *délégué du personnel* the burden of my new responsibility felt ominously light. I was first congratulated on my appointment, along with Sarah, in Madame Suger's office over a glass of Institute champagne. (Institute champagne was indefinably different from other champagnes. There was always a quid pro quo suspended invisibly among the bubbles.)

Madame Suger, raising her glass, said she hoped we could all work happily together in pursuit of the general good. As far as the first week went, and apart from the fact that Sarah dusted down her old portable typewriter and bought a new ribbon for it, that was that. I couldn't help seeing it as a symbol of something: the fact that we had an ancient portable typewriter at our disposal, while Madame Suger could avail herself of the Institute's computer Behemoth. Like David and Goliath, perhaps.

In the second week things began to hot up. The typewriter was put through its paces. It produced a dignified letter requesting clarification of the Institute's precise attitude to adult students who wanted to smoke in class.

'I'm sorry,' said Sarah, handing me the letter in draft. 'The typewriter's an English make. You have to put the accents in by hand. Will you check I haven't missed any?' Madame Suger spoke perfect English. Nevertheless it was *de rigueur* that all communication with her took place in French. It was her country after all. As Sarah's written French was vastly more polished than mine was it had been decided that she would actually compose the letters. Besides, though neither of us mentioned this, her typing was better too.

Madame Suger responded graciously on three sides of paper, managing to take three separate positions on the issue which overlapped without exactly contradicting each other. As a preliminary exercise in getting the measure of the other side this exchange was not without value. But it was in the third week that things began to get interesting.

'It's just got to be a strike. It's the only way.' This was the opinion of George, delivered through the cloud of cigarette smoke that had been generated by a fair number of teachers during an impassioned half hour in the *salle des profs*. George was one of the more ebullient personalities among the staff. Presumably ebullience had come in handy the day he had rediscovered, in this very room, the wife he had left America to get away from. ('He that loseth his wife shall find her,' as Malcolm had biblically put it.)

'Do you really think a strike's the best solution?' asked Sarah.

'The Métro and the SNCF do it often enough and to good effect,' said someone else, backing George. 'You know, just one day at a time. A brief inconvenience but one that shows muscle.'

'But we're not the Métro or the railway.' I piped up for the first time. 'Just look at us. This organisation has thirty competitors in Paris alone. If we start getting strike-happy the clients will go elsewhere and the institute will cut down on...'

'Then we'll go to the other ones,' George intercepted the argument. 'They'll be needing more staff to deal with the upturn. What's wrong with that?' He inhaled slowly on the cigar he had been gesturing with during the discussion and blew a new cloud of smoke across the table.

'It's not so simple,' said Sarah, 'as you well know. Employers aren't necessarily going to favour staff from a place with a record of strikes.' There were a few supportive nods from around the table and more smoke was exhaled into the thickening atmosphere.

'And also,' I followed up, 'how could we ever get unanimity? It's not like the Métro. Everyone knows everyone else for one thing. Individual people may have special reasons not to join. Families to worry about.' I was taking a gentle swipe at George. 'That kind of thing. A partially supported strike would be a disaster. It'd play right into their hands, split the staff down the middle for ages to come.'

George looked round the table and took his cue from the number of heads that were almost imperceptibly nodding agreement with me.

'Well, all right, David,' he said. 'Have it your way. But you've given yourself a tough job to do. Getting a deal out of Suger over the coffee cups won't be child's play. But there you are. It's up to you. You're our representatives. Get in there and do something. But let's keep the strike option open – for if you fail. OK?'

Sarah and I promised to do what we could and then the meeting broke up. But it was hard to know how to crystalise a miasma of discontent into precise demands for improvements. In the end Sarah typed a letter, to which I added the accents, which informed the management … that the staff were unhappy with the irregularity of their lunch breaks.

Two days later Madame Suger, Rebecca, Sarah and I were seated in a perfect square at Madame Suger's round table. I felt decidedly nervous and even Rebecca seemed a little less assured than usual. But Madame Suger, in a shoulder-padded suit that managed to look both chic and sensible, with gold pendant earrings and with her honey-coloured hair coiled high on her head, was a picture of serene confidence. 'Well now,' she began with a gentle smile, 'what can we do to help?'

With exaggerated civility, and speaking in French, I outlined the cause of complaint, laying equal stress on the diminished efficiency of staff who did not have proper breaks and on the human discomfort caused to them. Madame Suger reiterated with equal civility her sympathy in principle and her inability to do anything about the situation in practice. Rebecca pointed out the dire consequences to the Institute of not being able to offer its services at certain hours in the middle of the day: lost contracts, redundancies, that sort of thing. 'Even the Métro, which has little competition, does not shut down for lunch.'

'They do have rather more than thirty staff,' Sarah pointed out.

'Well then,' I said, 'let's come to another point. The staff have asked me to put it to you that time spent travelling to work should be regarded as part of the working week and paid accordingly.'

Sarah flashed me a quick look of surprise mingled with anxiety. This was certainly not on the agenda:

nobody had ever put forward such a bizarre proposal. A faint look of horror crossed Madame Suger's composed features, but momentarily, as a wind ripples a cornfield. Then she regained control of them. 'All travelling time?' she asked incredulously.

'All travelling time,' I said.

Rebecca intervened. 'That just isn't possible, David. No organization in the world pays its employees to travel in to work. Surely you must know that. You might decide to commute from London – or Vancouver.' She laughed. A little nervously, I thought.

'It's just not on,' said Madame Suger. 'You don't need to be an accountant to imagine the cost. You must learn to be a little realistic in your demands.'

'I suppose,' I said, 'I might be able to persuade them to moderate their claim for travel payments if they felt some progress had been made on the lunch front.'

Madame Suger swallowed, setting her earrings aquiver, and was silent for a moment before she replied, 'Perhaps we could make a token gesture. But then I'd need to ask in return for some extension of *disponibilité*.' Disponibilité meant the number of hours each week during which each staff member was available for work.

I drew in a deep breath, wished myself luck, and said, 'I think that if you could guarantee an hour's minimum lunch break, to include a maximum of twenty minutes travelling, they might drop the travel money claim altogether.'

Madame Suger's neatly plucked eyebrows moved expressively upward. 'Guarantee, no,' she said. 'That would be impossible. But perhaps we could undertake to make every effort to ensure that the condition were met.'

I came back. 'That would only be acceptable if you were prepared to back it up with a penalty payment – say one hour's pay – on the rare occasions when the condition could not be met.'

'Then could you guarantee five additional hours' *disponibilité*?' Madame Suger asked.

'Five?' I said.

Madame's head shook, and her earrings swung a bit.

'Too much. Two.'

'Not enough.'

I thought of Ian. I wanted him to be proud of me. I took another deep breath, crossed my fingers under the table, and went on. 'Remember,' I warned, 'I'm going to have a hard time getting them to drop the travel question.'

Madame Suger and Rebecca exchanged glances. 'Two and a half, then,' said Madame Suger, probably not enjoying, in her own office, a sensation she might previously only have experienced when shopping on holiday in Morocco. Sarah and I nodded to each other and the meeting was over, the deal done.

Sarah and I walked out into the corridor together. I had the feeling she was torn between feeling angry with me and being impressed. I sensed her trying to steer between the two. 'You might have told me what you were going to do,' she said once we were outside. 'We're supposed to be a team. How can anyone work with you when you go off at a tangent like that?'

'I didn't know,' I said, 'until the moment came, and then it was too late to check with you. Anyway, it worked, didn't it?'

Sarah had to admit that it had.

I said, 'Anyway, I've always suspected you had psychic powers. Thought perhaps you'd know what was going to happen in advance anyway.'

Sarah shot me a sideways glance. 'Whatever gave you that idea?'

'Only joking,' I said.

Sarah decided to be emollient. Perhaps she was beginning to like me. 'Anyway, I'm pleased with the result. You seem quite clever after all. But for God's sake don't tell any of the others what you did. Otherwise they really will ask for travel money and who knows what else besides. You'll have made a bed of nails for us both.'

I looked at her. The idea of a shared bed of nails did not appeal. We went for a coffee instead.

When we'd sat down with an espresso in front of each of us Sarah fired her bolt. She peered at me narrowly and said, 'I do know what that little exhibition of bravado was all about. We're lucky there's a young man in your life you're trying to impress.'

'Bloody hell!' I said, extremely startled. 'How do you know it's a man and not a woman?'

'I just know,' she said. 'Are we likely to meet him any time soon?'

'He's coming over from London at the weekend,' I said, and I heard my voice go bashful and quiet.

Sarah gave me a wonderful smile at that point. 'I think that's just great,' she said.

TWENTY-THREE

A letter arrived from Jean-Charles. I'd written to him as soon as I'd arrived in Paris, to give him my new address. His reply, written in an astonishing copper-plate hand, filled, though on one side of the paper only, six sheets. I was touched and flattered by its length.

He told me that the weather was still holding up in Provence. Though we were in late September now it was still hot down in the south. It wasn't that cold in Paris actually, but I still envied him that extra bit of heat. Then he got down to the important part.

After I had left his house that Sunday Raoul had stayed with him. Jean-Charles hadn't felt able to turn him out, although Raoul had insisted, in writing, that he was more than prepared to leave, as he didn't want to cause any problems between Jean-Charles and his parents.

I was bolstered by Raoul's presence in the house, Jean-Charles wrote. *He gave me strength. Though as the day wore on I became so frightened about what was going to happen I thought I was going to be sick. I felt as ill and as near to dying as you do when you've eaten a bad oyster.* That was a very French comparison, I thought. I who had never eaten an oyster, not even a good one.

Then my parents arrived in the evening. I was

suddenly calm and in control. I said I had a friend over, and could he stay the night? I presented Raoul to my parents, explaining that he couldn't speak. I told them he was a talented painter, and got him to show my parents his sketch book. They said, of course he could stay the night. They talked about getting a room ready. That was when I knew I had to do it. I took a deep breath, then told them that he had stayed with me the previous night, and that he'd shared my room. (I didn't say 'my bed'. They knew there was only one bed in the room. I didn't need to spell it out.) I said I wanted to do the same tonight.

My parents looked as shocked as if I'd hit them both with a hammer. My mother recovered first. If that's what you both want, she said – and she looked very closely at Raoul's face as she said the word 'both' – it's all right by us.

Jean-Charles's letter went on a bit after that. The main thing was that Raoul was now a fixture in the house. His parents were a bit uncomfortable about telling friends and family about the new arrangement and what it clearly implied about the sexual orientation of their only son, but, as he said, one things at a time. *Une chose à la fois.*

I wrote a long letter back to Jean-Charles, getting a lot off my chest about Ian and the way I felt. I told him Ian was coming to Paris at the weekend. I could feel my own excitement in my chest as I wrote that.

I travelled out to Roissy Charles de Gaulle on the RER. I actually saw the British Airways flight come in. It was just a speck in the sky at first. It seemed a very fragile, small thing. It made my mind boggle to think that this dot could contain something as solid and real, something so massively important, as the idea and physicality of Ian.

I saw him before he saw me. The door out from the customs control area was constantly opening and shutting, and gave a blinking view of the stream of people making their way out of the nowhere land of airport-airside and onto the solid territory of France. Ian was in the middle of that stream when I glimpsed him, backpack on shoulders and – the thought nearly made me cry – making his way towards … me.

We hugged. That is, he hugged me and I hugged his backpack. Our cheeks brushed but we didn't kiss. We talked about his flight, and about our imminent journey into the centre of Paris.

I showed him how to buy Métro tickets from the machine. He insisted on paying for them himself. I let him do that. I'd paid for his flight. He needed to reassert his independence, at least a little bit.

The RER took us to the Gare du Nord, from where we'd take the slow, stopping Métro line to Place Blanche. At least in principle. Our RER stopped at a signal in the tunnel, though, and we waited half an hour. At last the driver opened the doors and announced that we were within easy walking distance of the Gare du Nord. Though if we took the opportunity to jump down onto the trackside and make our way along it, it would be at our own risk. Ian and I looked at each other, exchanged a smile, and jumped. So did nearly everyone else.

This wouldn't have been possible on the regular Métro or the London Underground: the tunnels are too narrow and the sides of the trains nearly brush the walls. But the tunnel we were in was a wide one. There was a two-metre width of ballast to walk on between the tunnel wall and the train. Once we were in front of our halted train the Gare du Nord appeared in front of us just a couple of hundred metres ahead. It appeared as a brilliantly lit archway towards which we made our way, a hundred or more silhouetted figures, in the dark.

I took the risk of putting my hand on the back of Ian's neck for a moment. 'I'm glad you've come,' I said.

His voice came back to me from his own little bit of darkness. 'I'm glad I'm here,' it said. Together we progressed through the darkness and into the light.

I took Ian to a restaurant I knew in the Marais. It was a favourite of Malcolm's friends Peter and Fabrice. They weren't there that evening. On balance I was glad of that. For the moment I needed some time with Ian alone.

Opposite me at a small wooden table, his face looked bewitching in the candle-light. I even liked watching him eat, which is probably a sign of being in love. The French language calls jaws *machoires*, which means mashers, and is pretty exact and blunt. In general, watching other people using them is not a pretty sight. We had steak that evening, and I even enjoyed the sight of him munching that.

I asked him what he'd like to see the next day, thinking he might say Notre Dame, the Eiffel Tower, or Montmartre. His answer surprised me. 'I'd like to go to Auvers,' he said. 'I've been reading up about Van Gogh.' Auvers, a little way outside Paris, was where Van Gogh ended his days, living first at Doctor Gachet's house, then at the Auberge Ravoux. Auvers was where his last canvasses were painted and where, in the wheat-field that was the subject of his final painting, he took his own life.

'Then that's where we'll go,' I said.

Bedtime came. I only had the one room, with one single bed in it. I made up a sleeping place for Ian. Cushions on the floor. A sheet and blankets. He gave no indication, either in speech or in body language, that he'd prefer to join me in the single bed, and I didn't suggest it. But I did do one thing. I asked him, 'Can I kiss you goodnight?'

'Of course,' he said, and smiled. Then he leant towards me, put an arm around my shoulder, I put one of mine around his shoulder, and we very briefly kissed. He gave me his lips though, for that brief moment, not his cheek. Even that was more than I'd dared to hope. We got into our separate beds, I put the light out, and we said goodnight.

In the morning it was raining. We didn't care. We had coffee and croissants on the pavement opposite the Moulin Rouge's stage door. We were sheltered under the café's awning, and watched the rain dripping off the edge of it, while we stayed in the dry. 'We're like birds sheltering from the rain under the big leaves of a tree,' Ian said. It was the first time he'd referred to us by using the word *we*.

We took the bus to the Gare du Nord. Ian would only be in Paris for a couple of days, and it seemed wasteful of that time to spend too much of it looking at the tunnel walls of the Métro. The bus took us through the colourful street markets of Barbès-Rochechouart – a place I'd only recently learnt how to pronounce. It was an immigrant area. It looked more like Tangier than Paris. Ian had been to Paris before, but he'd never seen this side of it.

Then we were on the train, nosing out of the city, through suburbs and into the countryside. Ian looked around the carriage at one point and, I think, took a guess that no-one near us would understand English. Then he popped his big question. 'How did you find out you were gay?' he asked.

I said, 'It's all tied up with Van Gogh, curiously enough.' Ian smiled at that. 'I didn't think, when I went down to Provence, following in Vincent's footsteps with Malcolm, that I'd gone to find myself. But apparently I had.' I looked sideways at Ian. A bit cautiously I added, 'It also had something to do with you, I think.' He made a little movement beside me, but he didn't speak. 'I met Jean-Charles, as you know. He showed me the photograph of you that he'd taken. A week later I left London again and went back. Jean-Charles was surprised to see me again so soon, but pleased. We talked about you, inevitably. Then one thing led to another. We spent an evening together. We went back to his place. We had sex…'

'I rather guessed that was how it was,' Ian said, deadpan. Then, still deadpan, 'I had sex with Jean-Charles too.'

'Somehow I'm not surprised to hear that either,' I said. Neither of us probed for details about the sex we'd had with Jean-Charles: the where and how and what of it. If we wanted to discuss that at some future date, all well and good. If not, well, that was fine too. For now we let the matter drop.

We arrived at Auvers, and it was still raining.

We walked the streets of the little town under the rain. We had no umbrella with us. There hadn't been much rain since I'd arrived in Paris and I hadn't thought of getting one yet. Nor had Ian thought to bring one with him from London. He was a nineteen-year-old, and, thank God, nineteen-year-olds don't do things like that.

Again I had the spooky sense of walking into one Van Gogh canvas after another. Here was that familiar row of cottages, there was that unique church. Opposite the church was the small walled cemetery in which Vincent's simple grave and that of his brother Theo lay side by side. A neatly trimmed growth of ivy covered them both, uniting the two brothers as they slept. There was another thing about the ivy. It had been planted as a cutting from the garden of Doctor Gachet. Doctor Gachet who had befriended Vincent. Doctor Gachet whom Vincent had painted – he'd painted his garden too. Doctor Gachet who had dressed his wounds after he had shot himself.

We went into the Auberge Ravoux, where Vincent had lived out his final months. Here he had breathed his last in his room upstairs on July 29th in 1890. Ian did a quick calculation. 'Ninety-nine years and two months ago to the day,' he said. It was not the most exact of anniversaries.

It was barely noon but we drank a toast to Vincent's memory. In Pastis. Which Ian had never tried before. We watched the clear liquid turn milky as the ice and water were added to it. Vincent would have sat here drinking Absinthe, but you couldn't get that now. Pastis tastes much the same as Absinthe anyway. We chinked our glasses, said, 'Here's to Vincent,' and made do with the drink we'd got.

One beer and one French hot-dog later we climbed the lane out of the village, past the church again and onto the lonely plateau where in summer, wheat-fields waved. There was no wheat now but fields of maize that whimpered under the rain's assault. It rains cords, they say in France but up on that desolate hill that day it rained like ropes that slanted from a predatory sky. Below us the village lay, a blur of blue, while the yellow-grey maize fields stretched towards Paris, not far off but unseen. Crows, unaware of the fame of their forbears, started out of the crop at our approach and it was then, there, that I caught hold of Ian's head, his soaked hair, and pulled him towards me. He didn't resist. I felt his rain-sopped face against mine and kissed it. He kissed me back. Then, in that place of portent, among the waving corn, the rain, the crows, we embraced tightly, fiercely, and kissed each other properly for the first time, realising in that moment what we had both wanted, without always knowing it, all along.

TWENTY-FOUR

We didn't talk much on the journey back down the hill, or even on the train back into Paris. We both had too much going on inside us, and although wonderful, it was all too complicated to be put into words so soon. The rain had just about stopped by the time we got to Paris, but we were still wet through and through. Our clothes, our hair…

As soon as we got back to my studio we took a shower. We took a shower. A Tardis of a phrase, that, with an awful lot going on inside it.

The shower in my small studio was in a recess in the kitchen, which was screened by a semi-opaque plastic curtain like the famous one in the Bates Motel in Psycho. It didn't do a fantastic job of keeping the water in its place. If I was at all energetic in my showering there would be water all across the kitchen floor. But there wasn't a bath-tub, or even a proper wash-basin. I'd got used to taking showers daily, and every day then mopping up the floor.

We undressed together. Last night we'd done this before going to bed, but done it back to back, the way straight friends usually do. This afternoon – as St Paul said in another context – we saw face to face. I'd seen Ian naked once before, when he'd jumped into the River Wear that time when we'd been out for a walk three or four years ago. And I'd seen that picture of him in the basement gallery in Arles. But this was Ian's first glance at the naked me.

What do you look at first when presented with a naked man? It makes no difference whether you're gay or straight. The answer's obvious. And so it was with us. Ian's dick was so shrunk by the rain that it looked as if it belonged to a much younger boy. It was nothing like it had looked in that magical photograph. I laughed and told him so. He grinned back at me. 'Then take a look at yours,' he said. 'Yours has shrunk to nothing too.' He paused and added mischievously, 'Unless it's always like that, of course.'

'Be off with you,' I said. 'Get in that shower.'

'And leave you shivering and wet while you wait?' he said. 'No way. You're coming in with me too.'

And so I did.

It was a tiny, cramped and inconvenient space. All the better for that, perhaps. We soaped each other down, of course. And watched each other's dick grow from strength to length.

Watching was not enough for us, it turned out. I took Ian's water-lashed cock in my hand, thinking how incredible this was, remembering I'd known him since he was an obstreperous school-kid, and slid his foreskin back and began to jack the shaft. He did the same with mine. I mentioned energetic showering. But that shower cubicle, at least since I'd been in the apartment, had seen nothing like this. The kitchen floor, invisible beyond the Psycho curtain, must, I thought, by now be inches deep.

We came quickly, almost simultaneously. Our semen joined with the warm rain of the shower that poured over us and turned it milky for an instant and then another and another one, until we'd emptied out. Some of the mixture ended on the kitchen floor, no doubt.

We turned the water off, then kissed and cuddled briefly – though for no longer than a second – and then got out. We towelled each other and put clean dry clothes on. I lent Ian a pair of jeans. They were ever so slightly short on him, but not so much that anyone would notice. He still looked all right.

Ian volunteered to mop the kitchen floor. I let him do it while I watched. 'Things I hadn't envisaged this time yesterday,' he said. 'Me in your kitchen, mopping up a load of water along with our combined spunk.'

Ian had always had a way with words. I may not have mentioned that.

We'd been invited to dinner with Malcolm and Henri. We climbed the steep incline of the rue Lepic. It wasn't till we were all together, the four of us, that I realised what a symmetrical pair of couples we were, though now it hit all of us. There were

Malcolm and I, both twenty-eight, and Henri and Ian, both nineteen. The two youngsters took to each other at once, and I was pleased – and I could see that Malcolm was also pleased – about that.

Ian was as startled and delighted by the walls of Van Gogh pictures as I'd been on my first visit. He was quickly in earnest conversation about them with Henri in a mixture of English and French. Halting French in Ian's case. While they were engrossed in that, Malcolm said to me, 'I get the impression there have been developments since yesterday. Am I right?'

'We went to Auvers together,' I said. 'On the Van Gogh trail, of course. We got very wet in the rain, so when we came back we had to take a shower together…'

'Got you,' said Malcolm, and grinned at me impishly. 'Enough said.'

There was smoked mackerel pâté with a fresh baguette. Then a casserole of guinea-fowl with mushrooms, onions and grapes. Brie and reblochon cheeses followed that. There were fresh peaches for those who still had room for them. To our surprise we found we all did. We sat up drinking in the salon till it was quite late. None of us were drunk, though a feeling of well-being suffused us all, for which the alcohol we were imbibing was at least a little bit to thank.

Ian and I took our leave around midnight and strolled back down the hill in the surprisingly warm dark. The cafés were closed now, except for the one or two big brash brasseries on Place Blanche. I toyed with the idea of taking Ian into one for a post-nightcap nightcap but in the end I did not. It would only have delayed the inevitable: delayed the moment when we found ourselves together in my bedroom. That paradoxically difficult moment for every new couple that have walked the earth. I imagine that even for Adam and Eve there must have been a moment like this. As I let us into the immeuble's big courtyard and then through the inner door and up the stairs I found I felt shy and nervous. Like a teenager. I guessed that Ian, who still was a teenager, must have been feeling the same thing but even worse.

Inside the studio I put the light on. It glared at us. Very gently we drew close to each other and, standing, started to kiss.

After a minute we slid apart again. 'Would you like a nightcap of any sort?' I asked.

'A glass of water would be nice,' Ian said.

'For me too,' I said. I was actually relieved by Ian's choice. Glad that I hadn't hit on – or been hit on by – a drunk.

We drank our water unceremoniously, standing by the kitchen sink. Then we went and sank together onto the bed. We started to fumble with each other's clothes.

'Thank you so much for coming to Paris,' I mumbled.

'Thank you for taking me to Auvers,' Ian said.

'And for everything that happened there,' I said.

'And everything that's happened since.'

'The shower was nice,' I said.

'And your friends are nice,' Ian said.

'I know,' I said. What else did one say at times like this? Then suddenly I found it coming out. 'Oh God,' I said. 'I'd better say this, and on my own head be the consequences. I think... No, not I think. Ian, I love you. It's as simple as... Oh shit!' I said. 'I didn't mean to say that.' I heard my voice buckle, then break, as those last words came out.

'Didn't mean to say it, or didn't mean it?' Ian asked. For a moment he was nine years my senior, not the other way round. 'Remember, I once said that to you...?'

'I'd hardly forget it...' I said.

'And I've been asking myself that question for the last two years,' Ian said, as much to himself as to me. 'What did I say? What did I mean? What part of it do I regret?'

I could hear his voice also now grow fragile. I realised

he was starting to get upset. I said, 'Don't regret anything, Ian. Something started then, two years ago, that neither of us was ready for. No regrets. Maybe we're ready for something now. Maybe still not yet. Let things take their course. We've all the time in the world ahead of us. There's no rush.'

He didn't answer. Not in words at least. He nuzzled his head in between my chin and collar-bone as if he had become a violin suddenly, and needed me to coax the music out. I stroked his hair. My hand the bow, his scalp the strings and fingerboard. 'OK,' I said. 'Let me be brave and stupid. I'll say it now and mean it. You don't have to say it back. I love you, Ian. I love you with all my heart.'

He started crying then. I felt his hot tears fall and run between my shirt collar and my chest. His whole body heaved and shook. He made no effort to change his position but just slumped on top of me. I stroked him, rocked him, held him till the tears and heaving stopped. Then my collar-bone picked up the vibration of his whisper. It came to me through the bones that were his bones and my bones, not through the air between us. *'I love you, David.'* And it was my turn to weep.

Sunday. Bloody Sunday. The day that shows you the seeds of its own destruction the moment you wake up.

I woke up in a single bed with Ian. His sleeping head was on the pillow beside me. I knew that I wanted to wake up and find it there every morning for the rest of my bloody life. Not just his head, though. I wanted his warm soft nakedness against mine. I wanted that smell of him I'd hardly known before last night. I wanted that proximity. I wanted that cock. Wanted those bollocks. I reached for them now. The bollocks were small and tight, the cock hard, hot and stiff. I had all those things now. Had them now but not tomorrow. Tonight Ian would fly back to England, the little tail-light of his aeroplane disappearing over the northern outskirts of Paris into the dark.

I had to wake him up. 'What are we going to do today?' I said.

He looked at me the way a puppy looks at you when it has just woken up. 'I don't know,' he said. 'But I know what we're going to do first.' I felt his hand come round my morning-sized dick. And so we tussled playfully beneath the duvet, and stroked each other's penis until, as we'd done in the same way twice before going to sleep last night, we brought each other off.

The sun shone from a canopy of unblemished blue. Paris sparkled clean after its yesterday's rain wash. We took the bus down to the river. We explored the Ile de St Louis and the Quartier Latin. We examined the water-colours that hung along the Pont des Arts. The day sparkled too, unblemished like the streets and sky. Yet it was an unexploded time-bomb. With Ian's departure a few hours from now my new world would end. The knowledge that we'd someday soon be able to construct it anew did not help at all.

We lunched expensively beside the Seine on a corner of the Place St Michel, watching the water running past, between us and the towers of Notre Dame. The water running past… We might as well have had an hour-glass on the table in front of us! We stroked each other's knees under the table. It was the best, in the circumstances, that we could do.

We had to change those circumstances. Short of my kidnapping Ian and keeping him here in Paris, not letting him return to university, there was only one thing we could do, and so we did that. We took the bus back to Place Blanche, went up to my studio, then took our clothes off and got into bed for two hours. We stroked each other to orgasm once during that time, but we both knew that wasn't the main thing.

'Don't come with me to the airport,' Ian said. 'I don't think I could cope with that.'

'I won't be able to cope with it either,' I said. 'But I'm coming anyway. I can't not do. Sorry but there it is. Not to come would mean parting with you a whole hour earlier than I need.' It was going to be bad enough whatever we decided to do.

We hardly spoke on the RER. Whatever was there to say? We parted at the departure gate. We kissed modestly. We were in a public space, after all. We stood tall and looked each other in the eye. 'I love you, David,'

Ian said.

I said, 'I love you, Ian.' I added, 'Come again very soon. You have to. I can't survive without you for very long.'

His eyes dropped away from mine. I saw only his long lashes as he said, 'Nor can I.' Then he beamed back up at me again. We smiled courageously. Neither of us was crying. He turned smartly away, and so did I.

I lingered in the terminal. I know I shouldn't have. I toyed with a coffee, then I had a beer. I watched the board. Saw his flight called. Go to gate. Boarding. *Dernier appel:* last call. When the time came I walked out of the building. I went to the place where the buses pull up and walked from there across some waste ground towards a distant fence. From here, through a gap between buildings, closed only by the high security mesh fence, I could see the runway.

After a few minutes I saw the British Airways 757 taxi out from the floodlit apron area and away across the dark field. Eventually it was just a pattern of lights among other patterns of lights, a mile away. It slowed, then turned and stopped. It seemed to wait an age, but at last it moved. The lights began to gather speed. Detached themselves from the other lights and rose into the air. The lights flashed in a complicated sequence that was impossible to fathom. They grew closer together, fainter, till they merged. At last the plane was a mere pinprick in the sky. I strained my eyes to follow it. Eventually the night's giant hand snuffed the light out –

snuffed Ian out as if he'd been a candle flame.

I broke up then. I banged the palms of both hands against the mesh of the security fence till it rang with the noise of a dozen cash-registers. Grief and rage coursed through my veins and my whole being shook. There was no-one near enough to see me. But even people hundreds of yards away would have heard me. They would have wondered what pain on earth was causing a grown man to bang on an airport perimeter fence, howling like a wolf against the night, raging against the dark.

TWENTY-FIVE

My success in extracting Madame Suger's reluctant concession over lunch breaks proved a mixed blessing. As far as I was concerned the most important thing to come out of it was the wide-eyed admiration of Ian when I told him about my unexpected success as a negotiator during that weekend. It was vain and foolish of me, I suppose, but I had put myself into that gladiatorial situation principally because – as Sarah had rightly surmised – I wanted Ian to be impressed, and to have some reason to look up to me. It was inevitable, I suppose, given that I was the older one. The trump cards of youth and beauty were in his hand, after all.

And also I had won much respect from my colleagues and found I'd considerably enhanced my standing in their eyes. The problem was that their expectations of me and the office of *délégué du personnel* were growing in proportion. Every other day now I found it necessary to work with Sarah on some carefully formulated letter or other, either to ask for clarification of management policies or else to make the inevitable demands for improved conditions. Mostly these skirmishes were no more than volleys of paper exchanged by Sarah's portable typewriter and Madame Suger's Goliath of a computer. But from time to time matters needed to be thrashed out at Madame's round table and these sessions involved careful thought and preparation: so much so that Sarah and I found ourselves spending almost as much time preparing negotiations for which we were not paid as the classes for which we were.

Malcolm thought that was a good thing, though. 'Keeps you busy,' he said in a spirit of tough love. 'Doesn't give you time to pine and mope.' He had seen how distraught I'd been following Ian's departure that Sunday night. Even though, with regular phone-calls in the days that followed, my pain – and Ian's – had been assuaged somewhat.

And in the end the results of my efforts and Sarah's seemed to make them worthwhile. I learned to be more disciplined in planning my strategies, going through all the probable moves and counter-moves with Sarah in advance. We successfully persuaded Madame Suger and Rebecca to institute a stand-by system of replacement for absentee teachers; this meant the end of the 'dawn raid' telephone calls from Rebecca from which we'd all suffered in the past. We also managed to elicit extra payments for preparation for classes with specialised needs. 'They want a lesson on the vocabulary of hedge funds,' one agonized teacher had complained the week before. 'You might spend a week looking for a book that dealt with that in English here in Paris.'

Madame Suger had seen the point in the course of an energetic discussion.

Another argument was over cancelled classes. Normally, if a teacher turned up for a class but the student did not, the teacher was paid and the school sent out its usual bill. But if notice to cancel was received forty-eight hours ahead the lesson was not billed and the teacher, who had not had to prepare or turn up, went unpaid. Occasionally though, the system failed and a teacher did not hear of a cancellation before arriving for a non-existent lesson.

'Teachers are always informed of cancellations by phone,' Madame Suger pointed out.

'Huck doesn't have a phone,' said Sarah. 'He came in twice last week for nothing.'

'If he doesn't think it worth his while to have one installed that isn't our problem,' said Rebecca. 'He could always get one of those mobile things.'

I pointed out that if all the teachers stopped answering their phones during the daytime for an indefinite period then Rebecca and Madame Suger would have a problem. It took only a few more minutes to come to a more satisfactory arrangement.

'What do you think's happened, David?' George greeted me on my arrival at work one day during the second week after Ian's visit. My heart sank. George only ever purveyed bad news.

'I've no idea, George,' I said wearily. 'They're selling Notre Dame to the States?'

'Very funny. This is serious. They've sacked Huck.'

I had to agree with George. That was serious. 'But why?'

'He didn't show yesterday.' Yesterday there had been a strike on the Métro.

'Lots of people didn't turn up yesterday. People who live out in the sticks. *Banlieusards* ... They're not going to sack everyone, are they?'

'Huck lives in the centre, less than an hour's walk.'

'Cecile lives less than half an hour's walk away. Are they sacking her too?'

'Course not. She's five months pregnant. You don't sack people for being pregnant. Not these days.'

'You're telling me they've sacked Huck because he has Aids?'

'Point of information. He's HIV positive; he does not have Aids. But you're about right. They say he's not physically fit for work. Because he can't walk four miles morning and evening?! Bullshit! It's a pretext, that's all. He's employed as a language teacher, not a goddam football coach. Fact is, they just don't want him around.'

'So what now, George? A worldwide strike of language teachers?' Two weeks before, I wouldn't have dared to speak to him like that.

'OK, OK. But somebody ought to do something. Or do you not agree?'

'Of course I agree. Only I don't happen to have any suggestions just at present. On the other hand I have got a stack of photocopying to do before eight thirty. That gives me ... seven minutes exactly. Can we talk about it at lunchtime? Where is Huck, by the way? Is he in?'

'No. They told him not to bother coming back. He phoned and told me. He only had the phone put in last week. Damn all good it's done him. And there's no rush for the photocopier, by the way. There's a notice on it: *Encore en panne.*' (Out of order again.)

'Merde,' I said. No translation required, I think.

Malcolm collared me during the coffee break. 'Have you heard?'

'About Huck? Yes.'

'What are you thinking of doing?'

'Me? What are you thinking of doing?'

'I've no ideas, David. It's you who's the *délégué du personnel*, ace negotiator, tribune of the proles....'

'Plebs,' I said.

'Suit yourself. Look, I'm not trying to tell you your job. It's just that not only do you come up with the bright ideas but you manage to get things done around here which is somewhat rarer. I'm sure you'll come up with something effective.'

'Well, if flattery can be a spur to creative thinking, I'm sure I will.'

'Or even shall,' suggested Malcolm. I punched his

shoulder in reply.

Owing to the indisposition of the photocopier, my class spent more time than usual that morning engaged in listening and writing tasks. It was during one of the latter that an idea came to me as I walked round the class, peering over my students' shoulders, suggesting here, correcting there. The students had been asked to compose a letter to a shop complaining about faulty goods. One of them had included the following: 'If you do not do nothing I would contact the press.'

'Belt and braces,' I said gently, pointing to the not and the nothing. 'One is enough. And use shall or will, not would. It's a real possibility so you want Conditional One, not Two.' But in my mind an idea was forming.

At lunchtime I made an appointment with Madame Suger's secretary to see the lady herself at three o'clock when, on this occasion, I would have finished teaching for the day. Until three weeks ago it had been possible to walk straight into Madame's office and beard her directly, but now the office space was so rearranged that I entered an outer office and was confronted immediately by the secretarial desk and the secretary behind it. Then there was a partition wall in which a closed door, exactly behind the secretary's back, led into the inner sanctum. This exercise in creative carpentry had been carried out at about the same time as Sarah and I became *délégués du personnel*. Whether there was any connection between the two developments I didn't presume to guess; the practical result was that, short of employing the most nakedly aggressive tactics, no-one could confront the President Director General without an appointment.

'And what can I do for you today, David?' Madame Suger motioned to me to sit down.

'I'm here on behalf of the staff,' I began.

'I didn't doubt it.'

'Sarah's working in company today. Otherwise she would be here too.'

'I didn't doubt that either.' She beamed and clasped her hands on the table in front of her. Gold bangles chimed like a tiny clock. 'Now tell me what is making you unhappy.'

I had rehearsed my part carefully, even trying over some of the phrases with a French colleague in the lunch break and polishing up on the use of the French subjunctive. I began, in brittle French, 'We are asking ourselves if the dismissal of Huck was not, perhaps, just a little hasty. We wondered if, in certain circumstances, it could not be reconsidered.'

Madame Suger leaned across the table. 'In what circumstances, for instance?'

'Perhaps it is for you, Madame, to suggest the circumstances.'

I was pretty sure that Madame Suger felt like kicking herself then. It showed in a slight hardening of her smile. She said: 'Unfortunately it is out of the question. We do not take the decision to dismiss a member of staff lightly or without long consideration.'

'I'm sure that's true,' I said. 'And that's why we beg you to make an exception in this case. Because, after all, you could not have considered for very long the fact that Huck was going to be absent from work yesterday. Not without a crystal ball at least.'

Madame Suger's smile was by now glacial. I thought of Ian, and the admiration I wanted to win from him. That gave me courage. I pressed my advantage home. 'Cecile hasn't been dismissed. Nor have Mike, Joanna, Clive, Richard or Duncan.'

'Huck was not dismissed for one day's absence from work. You know that very well.'

'Then you dismissed him because he has a non-notifiable medical condition. Is that it? Something which does not impair his teaching and which, as far as my experience goes, can not be transmitted in the course of normal classroom activities.'

Madame Suger was not amused. 'I consider his health renders him unfit for the stresses to which his work subjects him. Teaching is an arduous activity as you well know, David.'

'Have you had complaints about his classroom

performance from the students?'

'Such matters are confidential; I'm not prepared to discuss them with you.'

I delivered the last of the grand, subjunctive-laden speeches I had rehearsed with my French colleague in the lunch break. 'We beg you, quite simply, to change your mind, that is all. For the sake of good staff relations and good morale. If you decided to reconsider it would not be judged a sign of infirm purpose but a gesture of humanity.'

Madame Suger got up from her chair and walked slowly over to the window in silence. The Eiffel Tower obtruded inappropriately on her reflection.

'No,' she said at last. 'I can't take him back. The situation would arise again one day. And if the clients became aware of his condition .... then that might create problems for all of us.'

I took a deep breath, thought of Ian, and reverted to English. 'In Britain there have been some similar cases recently that have reached the newspapers. The press has had a field day. It hasn't always been good publicity for the employers concerned.'

Madame Suger turned slowly round from the window and said, also in English: 'Are you threatening me, David?'

I paused for a moment before replying thoughtfully, 'Yes, I do believe I am.'

Madame Suger turned again and gazed at the Eiffel Tower as if to draw strength from its example of resistance to the pressure of the wind.

She said, 'For a cautious man like you, David, that would be an extraordinary tactic to adopt. Quite out of character.' She thought for a second. 'Though maybe not. I sometimes wonder about the nature of the men I employ here. And I wonder if you would all react in such an extreme way if Huck had been found to have cancer or multiple sclerosis. However, as your story about the British press goes to show, the Aids question provokes exceptional reactions in many quarters. I can not deny that. David, I will consider very carefully what you have told me. Very carefully indeed.' She turned and faced me once more, her features again composed in a smile, though this time the effort of it showed around the eyes. 'And now I am sorry but I have another appointment.'

A few minutes later I had to call on Rebecca to collect the file on a new group of students. 'I'm glad it's you who's teaching them,' Rebecca said as she handed over the information sheets. 'It's a new contract and I want to feel they're in safe hands.' Then her voice changed key, a habit it had; the effect was as startling as anything in Schubert. 'Remember that no-one is indispensable, David. Not even our best teachers. Not even me. It's just as well you're such an asset in the classroom.' Then she flashed me a smile that unexpectedly twinkled. I couldn't decide what was behind it: a feeling of having scored a point or one of covert admiration. Certainly

Madame Suger had been quick off the mark with the internal phone.

'You're coming to dinner with us this evening,' Malcolm said when I met him in the café an hour later. 'We've got to call by the café' – he meant his local one in rue Lepic – 'to borrow some more cutlery. Huck's coming as well and we don't have enough knives and forks.'

'Huck coming to dinner? That's a bit of a first, isn't it?' Huck socialised little as far as I knew. Certainly I'd never found myself at the same dinner table as him. Meeting him today would be especially awkward. 'What's the occasion?'

Malcolm didn't answer that directly. 'It's a casserole of wild boar. Henri's in charge of the preparations, thank God. Listen, do you know they've reinstated him?'

'Henri?'

'Huck, dingbat. They rang him and told him it had all been a misunderstanding. He'll be back at work tomorrow. Don't know how you swung it but whatever you did it worked a treat. They're frothing mad with you down at the fun factory – so George said, anyway. Anyway, have a beer…'

TWENTY-SIX

'That's brilliant,' Ian said, down the phone-line that evening, when I told him about my triumph. 'You're a star. And, hey, listen, there's another thing. I've got a few days clear at the end of next week. I could come over, if you liked.'

Yes, I liked. I more than liked. In my eagerness my thoughts jumped ahead. 'That's wonderful. Maybe ... just maybe, I could wangle a few days off myself and we could go somewhere. Provence, perhaps...'

'That would be fantastic...' Words like fantastic, wonderful and brilliant, plus a few exuberant swear-words made up the greater part of the rest of that conversation. I promised to see if I could get some time off, and we'd talk again next day.

'We all owe you,' Malcolm said, when I discussed the new possibility with him. 'If we all offer to do an extra couple of hours – I mean there's thirty of us – that'll have you more than covered, and they can't possibly say no. I'll have a word with everyone.'

And he did. Dear old Malcolm. And everybody said yes most willingly. Dear old everybody else. I got Rebecca's clearance to take four days' unpaid leave, two on either side of the following weekend.

It was like watching video on rewind. A star appeared in the east. It was dusk and the landing plane's light looked grand and bright. The light strengthened, wings and fuselage materialised behind it. They were the things that bore up, enwrapped, cocooned and held safe the most precious cargo on the planet. I found I could barely breathe until I'd seen the fragile container of my heart kiss the earth with a tiny magic puff of smoke.

I couldn't keep my hands off him when we met. And he couldn't keep his hands off me. We hugged and kissed so needily, so energetically, so fulsomely in the arrivals hall that people turned and looked. Even on the RER and the Métro we sat thigh pressed close against thigh, and stroked each other's leg-top for a second or two every time the people sitting opposite us looked away at anything else.

In bed that night we burrowed with our cocks between each other's legs. We didn't try to fuck each other. I hadn't found out yet if Ian wanted to do that. It didn't matter either way. Certainly not tonight.

In the morning we took the train to Avignon. I'd phoned Jean-Charles and told him of our plans. We wouldn't be asking for accommodation in his parents' house, I'd said. We'd find hotels on our travels. But we would want to meet up.

It was lovely to travel from the tepid autumn weather of Paris, as the minutes and hours passed, into the warmth and brightness of the south. Along the valley of the Rhone the grape harvest was still in progress. Bright-coloured tractors and harvesters roamed the vineyards, unscrewing – that's what it looked like – the black bunches from the vine-stocks and piling them into carts, where they glistened like caviar.

We had dinner that evening inside the antique shop where I'd first gone with Malcolm. Again there was just one dish on the menu. A rich stew of wild duck in red wine this time.

We walked back from there along the side of the stream that ran in a channel by the road. We could see the *lavoirs,* the stone slabs in the water on which, until not so long ago the inhabitants of Avignon had pounded their washing clothes with poles. I put an arm around Ian's shoulder. It was dark now, though still warm, and there were few people about. 'We've never fucked each other,' I said, bringing the subject up a bit abruptly. I'd let our beautiful surroundings do the soft talk.

'No,' Ian said. 'I have fucked boys in the past, though. And been fucked.' Then he wriggled slightly under my arm. 'Boys is an exaggeration. Just one boy in each case. The same boy in fact.'

'Much the same as me,' I said. I told him about the threesome I'd had with Jean-Charles and Raoul. I gave him all the details. I'd got the feeling that he wanted that, and it turned out that he did.

'That sounds good,' he said. 'Do you think, when we get there, we'll end up in a foursome at some point?'

I felt a frown pinching my face. 'Do we really want

that? Now that we're a couple, and they're a couple…'

'No, perhaps not,' Ian said. Though he said it a bit reluctantly, I thought. As though I'd shamed him into saying it.

'Anyway, you've had sex with Jean-Charles.' And now I couldn't resist asking, 'Was he the guy who fucked you and who you fucked?'

'No,' Ian said. 'That was someone else. Tell you another time.'

'So with Jean-Charles…?' I prompted. We were both getting excited, I realised. Another minute and we'd want to get each other's dick out.

'I was larking about by the river with the two other guys I was on holiday with. We were all naked…' I told him I knew that bit.

'The others didn't want their photos taken. But they sat on a rock and watched while I posed for Jean-Charles. To make me laugh they started playing with their cocks. Seeing that made me get half hard, as you saw in the photo. They saw that, and it spurred them on a bit. The thing is…' He paused for a second as we continued to walk along the streamside. 'The thing is, even if you start playing with your dick as a joke, it pretty soon becomes more than that. Mine got fully hard after that and, not to be outdone by the others, I started playing with it.

'At that point Jean-Charles, the only one with shorts

on, undid them and dropped them, showing us his own hard prick. By now we knew we were all going to go for it. Jean-Charles took his shorts right off, and stood there in just his socks and boots. We others had bare feet. We came close to one another, then standing in a circle by the edge of the river, all wanked – some of the time doing ourselves, sometimes reaching across and, well, you know…'

'Wow,' I said. I found myself picturing the scene only too easily. 'That's the bit J-C did *not* tell me.'

'The post-script to that,' Ian said, 'was that, although the three of us boys had never touched each other before or even thought about it, after that we all wanked each other when we went to bed – every night for the rest of the holiday. Not that the others were really gay. In their case it was just high spirits.'

'And was either of them the boy you first fucked with?' I couldn't resist that.

Ian giggled. 'No. I hadn't done that yet. That was much more recent.'

I decided to let it go at that. I wanted him there and then. In a doorway perhaps… We were passing a bar at that moment. It was brightly lit. There were no dark doorways in sight. I decided to be prudent. 'Why don't we go in and have a drink?'

It was a nice bar. Full of bare stone walls, a log fire, and atmosphere. We only stayed for one quick beer, though. We had other things to preoccupy our minds and hearts.

Back at our hotel we could hardly wait. All the way upstairs we were fondling and groping each other. Yes, we had been together in bed as recently as last night. But before last night it had been a fortnight, and we hadn't really caught up yet. We took our clothes off in a frenzy. I knelt at Ian's feet and started dementedly to pull on his cock with my mouth. He stopped me – pulled me off him by the hair on my head, almost. 'Shit, I'll come too soon,' he said.

I laid him on the bed, on his back, noticing approvingly the stiffness of his six-inch cock. And then I remembered something. My heart sank into my boots. 'I didn't bring condoms,' I said.

'I did,' said Ian, a little shyly. 'They're in my backpack.'

I laughed my relief. 'You little fox,' I said.

He wasn't as easy to enter as Raoul or Jean-Charles had been. He was less practised, of course. He'd only been done the once (same as me!) and I had to go slowly and gently, even with my modest-sized dick. (Though Ian was an inch or two taller than me, when it came to our dicks we were pretty much of a muchness, both as to girth and length.)

My patience was rewarded. He relaxed, and I massaged the inside of him gently with my penis, while his soft inner tubing slid my foreskin back and forth.

He came almost at once. I'd barely had time to feel for his penis before he clutched at it himself and tugged it briefly, immediately squirting white plumes of semen up his chest.

But that was all the stimulus I needed, apparently. I felt my own fountain rise within me and found myself starting to pound away at him in the manner of a much rougher-behaved chap. I only just had time to say, 'Are you all right with this?' before the time came when it made no difference whether he was or not. I felt myself empty out inside him in spurt after spurt.

I didn't pull out of him. Neither of us wanted that. We pulled the duvet up over us – a bit of a contortionist's trick, that was, in the circumstances – and dozed a little, while still plugged together by my slowly dwindling cock. We unplugged eventually in the small hours, and I took the condom off. Then we had to get up and piss, which we hadn't done before going to bed. We watched each other doing that with mild enjoyment and then, like good boys, cleaned our teeth. We slept cuddled closely together, then. Tummy pressed against tummy, and spent cock against spent cock. Throughout the night they both incontinently dripped.

In the morning we toured the Palace of the Popes. We saw the hall where Antipope Benedict XIII had held court, sitting between two roaring fires to ward off the ague that was spread by mosquito bites. I told Ian the story of the bites that Malcolm and I had suffered in Avignon back in the summer. 'Pope or Antipope,' I said. 'he has my sympathy on the mosquito front.'

We walked out to the garage on the ring-road, where Malcolm and I had got the clapped-out hire-car. 'I wondered,' I said when we go there, 'if you still have…'

They had. We rented it.

On the road to Arles I took advantage of that driving situation – the one in which you can't eyeball the other person, or be eyeballed back – to ask Ian a question. 'It's very easy to see why I'm crazy about you,' I said. 'You're nineteen and I'm twenty-eight. What I can't get my head round … is that the reverse also seems to be the case. I mean I'm humbled by that and gobsmacked. But…'

Ian took his time about replying. At last he said, 'Complicated, that one. But isn't everything in life? You weren't gay when I first knew you. Now you are. I'm having a bit of difficulty getting my head round that one. Although it's very nice, of course… Me and you, though…'

I took one hand off the steering-wheel and rubbed his thigh with it. 'You and I,' I said. I'd been his English teacher once.

'I just looked up to you. Don't know why. I had lots of teachers. All facing up to us lot every morning. We were a rowdy lot. It must have been a brave thing for all of you to do, now I look back on it.'

'It was just a job,' I said.

'But you struck me as the bravest of the lot of you.

Funny… Don't know why I thought that.'

I said, 'Did you fancy other men in their early twenties when you were just fourteen?'

'A few, perhaps,' said Ian. 'Not many. None more than you.'

The rear-view mirror, which was anchored to the windscreen by a not very efficient suction pad, now took the opportunity to slide snail-wise down the glass. Ian captured it with a hand and stuck it back up.

'You were clever, brave and handsome,' Ian said. I was shocked, knocked for six, by that. I'd never thought of applying any of those adjectives to myself. Neither, until this moment, had anybody else.

'I'm duly humbled,' I said, and I meant it. 'From this moment on I'll try and live up to that.'

'Until forever?' Ian queried.

'Is forever what you'd like?' I asked.

'Yes,' he said.

I don't know why but I felt suddenly angry with him. I tried not to show it, but failed in the attempt 'You don't know that,' I said. 'You're just a kid.' I tried to soften it, but it was another failed attempt. 'King Lear, remember. *He's mad that trusts in the tameness of a wolf, a horse's health, a boy's love*…I'm twenty-eight. I can't help thinking that.'

He lost it and suddenly bawled his eyes out. I had to stop the car and sort him out. Sorting him out meant a kiss and cuddle and my saying sorry about a hundred times, with tears streaming down my cheeks as well as his. I hadn't expected this morning to be like this.

Jean-Charles had found us a cheap hotel near the Place du Forum, and after we'd checked into it we met, the four of us, in the café there. The one that was painted by Van Gogh. 'It heightens the atmosphere a bit, doesn't it?' said Ian, looking about him as we sat on the terrace in the spilling yellow light. 'I mean, knowing that this was the very place.'

It also heightened the atmosphere to know that the last time Ian and Jean-Charles had said *au revoir* to each other they had just had sex. And that the same went for me and Jean-Charles, and Raoul as well. None of us mentioned any of that. In Raoul's case, of course, in order to comment he would have had to write a note on a piece of paper. He did not. He gave me a beautiful smile, which spoke volumes, instead.

We spent much of the weekend together. Ian and I, Raoul and Jean-Charles. I learnt that Raoul's paintings and sketches were beginning to sell. It helped that he now had an address and a phone number, even if he couldn't actually speak on the phone himself. It also helped that, with a roof over his head, he could keep his finished and unfinished canvasses dry. There was talk of his having an exhibition at the gallery within the next six months.

There were moments – I could feel them coming on, then feel us surfing through them – when the idea that the four of us might all get it together in bed seemed wonderful to all of us. Yet we didn't go down that road in the end. What happened in bed between Ian and me – yes, that is correct; trust me; I'm an English teacher – was in the end so much better than anything that might have happened among the four of us. I've no doubt the same went also for Jean-Charles and Raoul. And for Ian and me, at any rate, it seemed to get better every night.

We drove out along the flat roads of Provence, and across the hills. To Cavaillon, where the melons grow so quickly it's as if they're being inflated with bicycle pumps. We bought pink-fleshed juicy garlic from roadside stalls. We made love in the yellowing, brilliant fields, among vineyards where the leaves were turning to sunset-red.

In Arles itself we went into the Roman theatre, a rising ring of stone slabs. The acoustics here were fabulous. Ian sat in the stalls while I declaimed a part of *To be or not to be* under the vaulting blue sky. Then we changed places and Ian did...

I couldn't believe what I was hearing when he began it. King Lear's last speech. The speech that he hadn't been able to get through when he was a schoolboy. When I'd had to rescue him. That had begun our friendship… Broken my marriage. Brought us to where we were now…

'And my poor fool is hanged! No, no, no life!

Why should a dog, a horse, a rat, have life,

And thou no breath at all? Thou'lt come no more,

Never, never, never, never, never…'

I ran to him. He was so alone, standing on that vast stone stage beneath the infinite sky, an imaginary Cordelia dead and weighty in his arms. I wrapped him in my arms. 'Let it go,' I said. 'You've got me now. You always will.'

We stood there and held each other a long time. On that spot where Roman actors had said their pieces and brought tears to men's and women's eyes two millennia ago. We didn't cry noisily. Just as well, that was. I shudder to think what that amazing acoustic would have made of that.

The next day we retraced our steps to Paris. When you're a tourist the first sight of the Eiffel Tower from the train window, across the featureless suburbs, gladdens your expectant heart. When you live in Paris, though, it has the opposite effect. The first sight of the Eiffel Tower makes your stomach sink, as you think – Shit. Back to work.

Only it wasn't back to work this time in my case.

When we got back into my studio and opened all those post-holiday envelopes that are mainly bills … I found there was one from Madame Suger. It told me in very elegant French, in a style that dripped with subjunctives, that I'd been sacked.

TWENTY-SEVEN

Ian wanted to talk about Happy in bed that night. Perhaps that was simply because he'd talked about everything else. He'd exhausted the subject of the disappearance of my job in two short sentences. 'Good. That means you can come and live with me in London.'

'Believe it or not,' I said, 'that's what I wanted to hear you say before I came to work in Paris in the first place.'

'Sorry,' Ian said. 'I didn't know my own mind back then. I do now.'

'The tameness of a wolf,' I reminded him gently, *'a horse's health…'*

'A boy's love,' he finished. 'Mine's the exception. You can count on that.'

At that moment I began to believe he meant it.

'I may not be able to come to London at once,' I cautioned. 'A few things to sort out here first.' I felt him stir uneasily in my arms. We were well wrapped in the bed-clothes. It was a cold night in Paris. I relented. 'But we'll be together soon,' I said. 'You can count on that.'

He rewarded me with a squeeze in the dark. It was then that he brought up the subject of Happy. 'I'm sure he knew the boy who went to prison,' he said. 'The one who was being blackmailed. I'm sure they'd met.'

'You have a lively imagination,' I said. It wasn't the first time I'd told him that.

'That was what he was going to talk to you about that night…'

'That doesn't make me feel good,' I said. 'I didn't let him talk, remember. I had an essay to write.'

'That's hindsight,' Ian said. 'Nothing that happened, or may have happened, was any of your fault.'

'It's always nice to be told that nothing is one's own fault,' I said. 'But some things have to be. That's what growing up is about.' I pressed him to me then, and rocked him gently. 'Growing up is hard to do, my precious.'

He said, 'If I can do it with you I'll be all right.'

I kissed him. I said, 'It's time you went to sleep.'

Madame Suger's letter had told me that because of a downturn in the Institute's fortunes it would be necessary to make some redundancies. Last in first out… That meant me, evidently. I would be paid a month's salary in lieu of notice. I would only need to return to the Institute to empty my *casier*. Ian's flight wasn't till the evening. I went to the Institute in the morning, taking Ian with me. I had nothing to lose by that. It would be nice to show him off to my fellow staff.

They loved him, of course. Especially Sarah. 'I knew

he'd be handsome,' she said. 'It was a feeling I kind of got.' She smiled at Ian approvingly. 'You must cherish David, Ian. He's good.' She turned back to me. 'There's something I ought to tell you. Huck's gone back home to America. He feels his condition's getting worse. He asked me to say goodbye from him – and a big thank you for what you did.'

Malcolm walked into the *salle des profs* at that moment with a thunder cloud of a face. 'I've just heard,' he said. 'I'm going to walk in to Madame Suger's office right away. There's going to be fireworks. We'll walk out, sit in, act up, you name it. You're going to be reinstated or there's going to be no more school left. Do you realise? After all you did for these guys they're not going to let you go under now.' He looked around the room and was rewarded by the sight of nodding heads. 'Madame Suger ought to be strung up!'

'Thank you,' I said. 'I wouldn't go overboard about the good I did for anybody. Huck's going back to America for one thing. So don't you go putting yourself out on a limb. I don't actually want to be reinstated as it happens. I'm going to join Ian in London.'

Ian, standing beside me, and momentarily tongue-tied, gave a little start. 'Really?' he asked. 'You mean that?'

'In a day or two,' I said. 'As soon as I've had time to pack my things and make arrangements about the flat.'

Malcolm looked astonished, though Sarah simply nodded. She seemed to know somehow that I'd want to do that.

Parting at the airport wasn't quite such a hardship this time, though it was still painful enough. I would be joining Ian in London two days from now. What I was going to do for a living I had no idea. But I would be living with Ian, sharing his bedroom, at his shared flat. That was the important bit.

I had dinner with Malcolm and Henri that night. They'd also invited their friends Peter and Fabrice.

Henri had done a starter of Puy lentils dressed with sweet peppers in olive oil, anchovies, lime zest and juice, which was followed by roast quail. I enjoyed it, but with a reservation. The reservation was that Ian wasn't there to enjoy it too. I knew I wouldn't enjoy anything properly until I was with him again. Our first meal together might be baked beans on toast or bread and cheese, but I looked forward to it already, as if it would be the greatest feast on earth.

Without Ian to share it with me I doubted if I would ever completely enjoy anything again.

But tonight's company was good. Fabrice and Peter were a couple in their late twenties, I guessed, and thought Fabrice was the older of the pair by a year or two. They'd been together about two years. In their company and that of Malcolm and Henri I was relaxed enough to wear my heart on my sleeve. 'I love Ian more than I've loved anyone before. And that includes my ex-wife. But in going back to London, jobless and penniless, throwing myself on him … especially with the nine year age gap … well, I just hope I'm doing the right thing.'

'There's nothing wrong with a nine-year age gap,' Malcolm said, and he and Henri exchanged a grin. 'You just have to remember that you'll have to make it up as you go along.'

'Every couple has to make it up as they go along,' Fabrice said, and Peter nodded his agreement. 'You won't be alone.'

Peter changed the subject suddenly. 'Have you ever heard Messien play?'

I had trouble with this. Mentally I tried to change gear. 'The composer? The one who transcribed all those bird songs?'

'I wouldn't say transcribed,' said Fabrice. 'It was more like he built great musical structure on the foundations their songs laid.'

'I see,' I said. 'But, heard him play…? No. Play what?'

Peter answered. 'He plays the organ in the church of La Trinité. Just behind where you live. You ought, before you leave.'

'We're going to hear him tomorrow,' said Fabrice. 'Want to come along?'

It was an extraordinary thing to find myself doing, on my last evening in Paris, my last evening before joining Ian in London - for good, I hoped, and certainly for better or worse. Attending an organ recital. It was a thing I'd never done before. And this one was being given by the greatest living French composer of classical music. Not just Peter and Fabrice were with me. Malcolm and Henri came too.

The sounds were beyond my comprehending. I knew nothing of musical structure or style. Ian, or maybe Happy, might have understood. But the grandeur of the music, its yearning and its passion, engraved themselves on my heart. I thought of my uncertain future and the muddle of my past, and found them echoed in the harmonies the great composer - who sat playing just a little way from us - had found. I felt then, safe among my four friends, that Messien was unwittingly giving me a glimpse of my own soul. And deep inside I saw something else there: I saw the future of Ian, and I knew then beyond any doubt that it was my job to help him shape that. I had the awesome responsibility of helping my beautiful boy grow into the man he would become.

Tomorrow life would begin for Ian and me. The challenge of that thought was as big and awesome as the music that echoed around the lofty vaults of La Trinité. But so was the confidence that suddenly filled me now. I felt stronger than I'd ever done. And yet with all of that I felt my chest begin to heave quietly and my tears silently run. I wasn't the only person to feel that, apparently. From either side of me a hand came, one Fabrice's, the other Henri's, and at the same moment each of them quietly grasped mine.

TWENTY-EIGHT

St-Rémy. Summer. 1997

The blackbird ceased his singing and dived into the darkness of the oleander bush in the corner of the garden.

As a garden it was small but as a piece of luck it was considerable. It would have been impossible but for the shop-cum-gallery, of whose ground floor premises it formed a part. The flat upstairs would have entitled us only to the view of it: of the red brick wall along which fig trees sprawled and lizards lazed, of the improbably tall and scrawny yucca that skewered its way skyward and of the cypresses that shed shade and bred blackbirds.

An item in the newspaper I was scanning caught my attention. 'Messien has died,' I said.

'I never got to hear him,' Ian said. 'Pity. But you did.'

'Yes. With Peter and Fabrice. The day I stayed behind in Paris to pack my things after you'd flown back. The day before I joined you for keeps. It was ... well, you know I'm not clever about twentieth century music. It was impressive.'

Ian was drafting a newspaper *annonce* for a new exhibition; it involved much crossing out, the knitting of his brow and the studious protrusion of his tongue from the corner of his mouth. He looked down again at his draft. 'Shall we say drinks are available, or is that asking for trouble?'

'I think people will assume that's the case anyway. No need to spell it out in neon letters.' I flicked a beetle from the newspaper. 'It says here they've found another gene.'

'Oh great!' said Ian. 'Like the gene that makes you gay. And the one that makes some people depressive. Soon they'll be able to have us all aborted before we can see the light of day. Think of all the adolescent angst that'll save. Down with diversity. *A mort la différence!* Though while they're at it, are they any nearer finding the gene that makes some people deny the truth of their own natures for up to twenty-eight years?'

'Ha-ha,' I said. That had been one of Ian's more irritating jibes at first. Now, after eight years, I hardly noticed when it was trotted out again from time to time. 'What time did they say they were arriving?'

'Malcolm and Henri? Between five and six, I imagine. They said they'd leave Monpelier after lunch.'

They lived in Monpelier now. Malcolm lectured at the university. Henri was marketing officer for the Hérault tourist board. 'They've come a long way,' I said.

'While we slog away selling artists' materials in the smallest specialist shop in Provence,' Ian said.

'You still don't mind?' I checked.

'Mind? In a place like St-Rémy?' Ian stopped. 'You always ask me that. I always give you the same answer. Pathetic, really.'

I smiled, mainly to myself. 'Hardly.'

'And tomorrow, what happens?' Ian asked.

'You're staying in to take a delivery in the morning,' I said firmly.

'Leaving you free to flirt with Henri.'

'No such luck with Malcolm about. And anyway, would I?'

Ian, who knew that I would, screwed up the sheet of paper he had been writing on and flung it at me by way of reply.

'Seriously,' I said, 'there are things to take care of. Noëlle isn't in tomorrow. And Malcolm and Henri will go off in the car, I guess. It's their holiday, not ours.'

Ian remembered something. 'There is another thing on tomorrow. Dinner with Jean-Charles and Raoul. The six of us.'

The blackbird reappeared from the bush and flew up into a cypress where he began a new, more solemn song, a lament perhaps for the dead composer who had once transcribed his wild music.

'You know,' said Ian, 'it didn't actually need Messiaen to write the blackbird's song down for the piano. Beethoven did it all in his third piano sonata.'

'You would say that, of course.'

'Of course,' said Ian. 'Did Happy never play it to you? The one in C.'

'Probably. You should know, anyway. You claim to know him better than I did.'

'Not literally. Mind you, we did live in the same town. Our paths may have crossed.'

'You were only eleven when he died. I didn't think even you were chasing older men at that age.'

'Don't be too sure. It has been known. But seriously, I do feel as though I knew him. We're so much a part of the same scheme of things. He had his picture of the night sky at St-Rémy; I have the real thing. He had a half-woken feeling for you while I... Well, there you go.' Ian broke off and gazed around the garden. 'I wish he could have come to St-Rémy and seen it for himself. He might have rediscovered himself – as a painter, I mean.' He looked straight at me, his head a little on one side. It was a look that I found irresistible; both of us knew it. 'Do you suppose,' he said, 'that we owe all this to him?'

'How do you mean?'

'That somehow we got here on his coat tails – because of his death?'

'That's morbid,' I said. 'Forget it.'

'I hope he's happy for us anyway.'

'And that's sentimental too, as well as being an unforgiveable *jeu de mots*.'

'Don't be so bloody English.'

'Then don't you go on maintaining the stupid fantasy that Happy was in love with me. You're as daft as Malcolm.'

'Just as well then isn't it? It took someone that daft to wait around long enough for you to make your mind up about who you were.'

'Waited around?' I objected. 'You were hardly unexplored territory by the time…'

'You know what I mean. Don't lower the tone.' Ian leaned back in his chair until it tipped right over. It was a party trick of his. He broke his fall with his hands at the last, precisely judged, moment and lay where he landed, draped across his fallen chair and moulded to its new contours as compliantly as if he had been a bundle of washing.

'You know,' he said, gazing up at the sky, 'I still sometimes try to imagine those last few minutes of Happy's. The ice still just thick enough in a few places. He steps onto it. Above his head the sky is a vortex of stars – like in Vincent's paintings, only this time it's for real. Everything is suddenly *en jeu*. You. The boy in the county court. (I'm still sure they'd met – to say the least; you'll say it's my tidy imagination.) Anyway, he looks down, and there is no ice any more, just a second infinity of stars, infinity multiplied by two. That is the last thing he sees. Then he takes his own place in the picture for ever.'

'You've too much imagination,' I said.

'And you've too little. You don't change.' Ian smiled at the sky. 'Mind you, I'm glad. Hey!' He got to his feet suddenly. 'I must go and get the baguettes before they run out. Do we need anything else?'

I said I thought not.

'By the way, Raoul sold another picture yesterday. One of his wheat-fields.'

'Good for him,' I said. 'Though I still can't see why people get so excited about his splodges. If he didn't label them wheat-fields nobody would guess. I liked his work better when he was doing his naturalistic stuff. When we first knew him. Still, I'm pleased he's making some money.'

'Maybe he's another fragment of whatever energy Happy left behind – the creative bit.'

'Oh cut it out. And anyway, Happy was a good draughtsman, not a splodger.' A memory stirred: Happy's history lecture notes, all composed of sketches of seals...

'So?' said Ian. 'You can never tell what people will turn into, given time and opportunity. Anyway, I'm off.' Ian went into the house. Seconds later I heard him leaving it by the other door into the street. I was left alone with the blackbird in the garden.

Five years in the south had tanned me deeply and any elfin quality I might have had was gone for ever. Ian, who boasted of what he called his 'nine years' juniority', still remained boyish in face and figure but we both knew that this could not last much longer; Provence's climate was hard on the complexion while its cuisine, though healthy, was not noted for its slimming properties. We both knew, and neither of us cared.

It had taken us a while to get to where we were. All those years ago, when I'd left Paris to join Ian in London, I'd found a job working in a pub. And there I'd stayed. We'd had a hard winter. Ian suffered some illness that left him barely able to walk for two months. He decided it was Aids, a legacy of an incautious university first year, but investigation proved it to be no more than an acute case of homesickness. He cured it by never returning home. For while my parents had been discreetly tolerant of their son's surprising change of life style, Ian's were the kind that love too much, desiring all possible good for their son except that he might have a different way of being happy.

We'd stayed together. We'd stuck it out. Ian completed that second year of his at university and then his third. I continued to wait at restaurant tables and work in pubs. Then we'd migrated south. And things had gradually fallen into place. The gallery inside St Rémy's charmed plane tree circle, where Raoul could show his work. With Jean-Charles to manage it. The art shop in the same building... We'd pooled our resources, Jean-Charles and I, and bought the place. We made a living, the four of us. Just. Unlike Raoul or Van Gogh, Ian and I would have nothing in the way of art to leave behind us – for all the beauty of our dreams. All that we had, all our experience, all our past, was invested in the brief present: a time and place that history might prove would be no more than a small window in the weather. Still, it was ours, never to be torn from us: our own vision, like Vincent's, of the sun.

THE END

****

Anthony McDonald is the author of over twenty novels. He studied modern history at Durham University, then worked briefly as a musical instrument maker and as a farmhand before moving into the theatre, where he has worked in every capacity except director and electrician. He has also spent several years teaching English in Paris and London. He now lives in rural East Sussex.

Novels by Anthony McDonald

SILVER CITY

THE DOG IN THE CHAPEL

TOM & CHRISTOPHER AND THEIR KIND

RALPH: DIARY OF A GAY TEEN

IVOR'S GHOSTS

ADAM

BLUE SKY ADAM

GETTING ORLANDO

ORANGE BITTER, ORANGE SWEET

ALONG THE STARS

WOODCOCK FLIGHT

MATCHES IN THE DARK: 13 Tales of Gay Men

(Short story collection)

Gay Romance Series:

Sweet Nineteen

Gay Romance on Garda

Gay Romance in Majorca

The Paris Novel

Gay Romance at Oxford

Gay Romance at Cambridge

The Van Gogh Window

Gay Tartan

Tibidabo

Spring Sonata

Touching Fifty

Romance on the Orient Express

All titles are available as Kindle ebooks and as paperbacks from Amazon.

www.anthonymcdonald.co.uk

Printed in Great Britain
by Amazon

49911093R00149